# HIS SUMMER SIDE PIECE

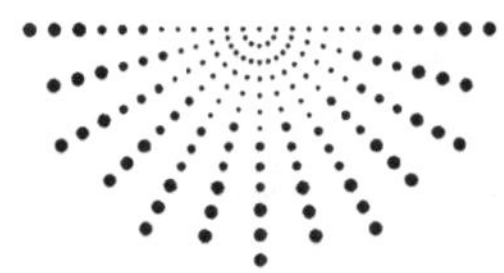

## KYIRIS ASHLEY

URBAN AINT DEAD

Email: urbanaintdead@gmail.com

Print ISBN: 979-8-9906748-0-6

# STAY UP TO DATE

To stay up to date on new releases, plus get information on
contests, sneak peaks and more,
Click the link below...
https://mailchi.mp/6d21003686d1/subscribe

# CONTENTS


*Soundtracks*     9
*Urban Aint Dead*     11
*Submissions*     13

Chapter 1     15
Chapter 2     24
Chapter 3     36
Chapter 4     44
Chapter 5     61
Chapter 6     74
Chapter 7     97
Chapter 8     106

*Review*     117
*Other Books By*     119
*Coming Soon*     123
*Books By*     125
*Stay Connected*     127

# Soundtracks

Scan the QR Code below to listen to the Soundtracks/Singles of some of your favorite U.A.D titles:

Don't have Spotify or Apple Music?
No Sweat!
Visit your choice streaming platform and search URBAN AINT DEAD.

Currently on lock serving a bid?
JPay, iHeartRadio, WHATEVER!
We got you covered.

Simply log into your facility's kiosk or tablet, go to music and search URBAN AINT DEAD.

# URBAN AINT DEAD

Like & Follow us on social media:
FB - URBAN AINT DEAD
IG: @urbanaintdead
Tik Tok - @urbanaintdead

<u>**Submissions**</u>

Submit the first three chapters of your completed manuscript to <u>urbanaintdead@gmail.com</u>, subject line: Your book's title. The manuscript must be in a .doc file and sent as an attachment. The document should be in Times New Roman, double-spaced, and in size 12 font. Also, provide your synopsis and full contact information. If sending multiple submissions, they must each be in a separate email. Have a story but no way to submit it electronically? You can still submit to URBAN AINT DEAD. Send in the first three chapters, written or typed, of your completed manuscript to:

URBAN AINT DEAD
P.O Box 448
Maybrook, NY 12543

*DO NOT send original manuscript. Must be a duplicate.*
Provide your synopsis and a cover letter containing your full contact information.
Thanks for considering URBAN AINT DEAD.

# CHAPTER ONE

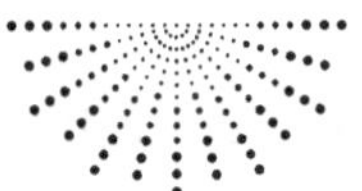

It was Memorial Day weekend, and the streets were filled with the smell of barbeque. Whisper had just gotten off of work and was excited about her three-day weekend. She pulled into the driveway of her small, two-bedroom home and said hello to her elderly neighbors, Mr. and Mrs. Johnston. They were outside sitting on the porch, drinking lemonade like they did every evening around five. They'd been in the neighborhood for over thirty years, and everyone loved and respected them.

Whisper made her way into the house and immediately took off her work clothes. As a realtor, she usually spent long nights in the office, working on the next closing. However, on this particular Friday, she hauled ass as soon as the clock hit five. Taking off her black pantsuit, leaving noting on but her white lace panty and bra set, she made her way to her en-suite bathroom. She ran hot water into her tub before pouring her pomegranate bubble bath inside. She placed her twenty-six-inch bundles into a high ponytail before going to her kitchen and pouring herself a glass of wine.

Once back inside her bathroom, she connected her Bluetooth and Junetober sang. She stepped down into the bubbly water, ready to relax. She'd not been in the tub for five minutes when someone began to knock at her door. Whisper rolled her eyes. She hated when people came to her house without calling first. Her phone began to ring, stopping Whisper's music, and she really became irritated.

"Damn, why can't people just leave me alone? I just want to relax," Whisper spoke aloud as she got out of the tub. Walking over to her phone, she looked down to see it was her best friend, Zariah.

"Hello," Whisper answered.

"Bitch, I know you hear me knocking on your door. Can you answer it? Damn."

"I'm taking a bubble bath. You would know that if you would have called first," Whisper shot back.

"Can you please just open the door? I really need to talk to you," Zariah pleaded.

"Give me a second and I'll be right down."

A few moments later, Whisper was opening her front door to let Zariah inside. When Whisper looked into her best friend's face, she instantly knew something was wrong. Zariah's eyes were red and puffy, so Whisper knew she'd been crying.

"Best friend, what's wrong?" Whisper asked in concern, hugging Zariah.

"Whisper, I can't take it no more. This nigga done got married. Why the fuck would he do that shit to me? I love that man so much, and all he does is play with me," Zariah cried, hugging Whisper back tightly.

"What? Who got married? Marco? I know you fuckin' lying. When?" Whisper asked, confused about what Zariah was saying.

"I don't know. A few days ago, I guess. He married his baby mama. I been down for this nigga, ridin' for him for seven fuckin' years, and he married her? I don't know what I'ma do. I gave this nigga my heart and soul, and he just played with it. He acts like I never meant shit to him."

"I'm so sorry, Z. I know how much you love Marco, so I know that shit hurts. But on the real, that nigga wasn't shit. That nigga was over there telling you he wanted to be in a poly relationship, just so you could have threesomes with him and other bitches. He's a narcissistic, manipulative asshole, and you deserve so much better. That nigga been trash."

"He was just misunderstood, and I tried to be the one to understand him, but that shit got me hurt. Why would he marry that girl?"

"How did you find out they had gotten married?" Whisper asked.

"I was scrolling Facebook, and somebody tagged them in a picture. It was a picture of them walking down the aisle after they'd gotten married. And the caption said, 'Mr. and Mrs.' When I seen that shit, my entire soul dropped," Zariah revealed as she shook her head.

"Wait, so this nigga didn't even tell you that he'd gotten married?"

"Hell no, he still don't know I know. He called me earlier, telling me he wanted to come over tonight."

Whisper shook her head. She couldn't believe the way some men treated women. Zariah was good to Marco and would do anything she could for him. Hearing stories like this made Whisper happy to be single. There were no men in her life claiming to love her while constantly publicly humiliating her, and she was proud of that.

"Girl, so what you gon' do? I know you not gon' keep fuckin' with that nigga, are you?" Whisper asked.

"I don't know, Whisper. I really love that man, and I just want to know why he did me like this. I thought we would get married and spend the rest of our lives together. But I guess Marco had other plans."

Tears fell from Zariah's eyes uncontrollably, and Whisper felt sorry for her friend. She walked into the kitchen and grabbed a bottle of Tito's and two glasses before making her way back into the living room.

"I was sipping on some wine while I was taking my bubble bath, but I'm sure you need something stronger."

"You right about that. You got some juice or something? I need a chaser," Zariah asked.

"Yeah, it's some cranberry juice in the fridge," Whisper replied.

The two friends had a few drinks while they spoke about Zariah's situation. Whisper hated that her friend was going through something so hurtful. However, she could tell from her conversation that Zariah was going to take Marco back. They spoke for a few more hours before Zariah left and headed home.

Whisper sat on her couch, scrolling TikTok. She came across a flyer for a rooftop day party downtown. It was scheduled for the next day, and Whisper shared the flyer with Zariah with a text saying, "We going." She knew her friend needed to get out, and she felt the party was just the thing. Zariah quickly texted back, telling her she would be ready. Whisper walked upstairs and ran herself another bubble bath, this time being able to relax.

THE NEXT MORNING, WHISPER WOKE UP AROUND ELEVEN IN the morning. She went down to the kitchen to make herself a light breakfast of toast and scrambled eggs. Zariah called her and let her know she'd be there around three, so they could go to the party together. Whisper agreed before finishing her breakfast and heading to her closet to find something to wear. She had tons of new clothes that she hadn't worn yet; half of the items in her closet still had tags on them. The hard part was finding something that would make a statement.

She settled for a pair of white fitted slacks with a blue, lace, halter bodysuit. Gold Fendi jewelry adorned her neck, wrist, and fingers, looking good next to her caramel complexion. She brushed her hair up into a ponytail before looking into the mirror, liking what she saw. She placed a pair of gold Louis Vuitton shades on her eyes before choosing her fragrance of choice. She sprayed Juliette Has A Gun's Not A Perfume all over her body, starting at her ankles and working her way up to her neck. When she was done, Zariah called to let her know she was at the door.

Whisper walked down the stairs, opening the door, letting Zariah inside. She wore a white Zara jumpsuit with gold accessories. The blonde bob she wore looked good against her chocolate skin tone.

"Bitch, you look good as hell," Whisper complimented.

"Thanks, girl, so do you."

Whisper and Zariah got into Zariah's Honda Civic and made their way to downtown Detroit. When they arrived at the venue, they walked inside and stepped into a small elevator that took them up to the roof. When they walked into the party, they walked over to the bar. Catching the bartender's attention, they ordered themselves a couple of drinks.

"I got this round," Whisper offered, reaching into her purse and pulling out her debit card.

Grabbing their drinks, Whisper pointed out a table, and they walked to it. "Girl, this shit a vibe. It's a lot of fine ass men in here," Zariah observed.

"Yeah, it is. Maybe you will find yourself a new one. Have you talked to Marco?" Whisper questioned.

"Yeah, I talked to him. He came over last night."

"Sooo, what did he say?"

"He said he didn't mean to marry her, and he doesn't want me to leave him. He told me he only married her because of their daughter."

"Bitch, what? What does he mean he didn't mean to marry her? How do you walk down the aisle and exchange vows and not mean to do it? That don't make no sense, Zariah."

"He says he only loves me, and I believe him," Zariah replied, sipping her expresso martini.

"If he loves you then why would be marry someone else, Z? Come on, friend. I know you not that gone over that dick? You lettin' that nigga play in yo face."

Whisper couldn't believe Zariah was allowing this. She didn't understand where her sense of self-worth was. Zariah was a beautiful woman with a lot to offer. Zariah owned a chain of restaurants called Seafood and Soul with four locations in the Metro Detroit area. She was well-known in the city and could have any man she wanted. Instead, she chose to stay with a man that married another woman behind her back. Whisper knew she couldn't tell her friend what to do. She just wished Zariah wanted better for herself.

"I just want to give him a chance. I don't want to let go too soon. I feel like he's going to realize that I'm the one he's supposed to be with. Or what if him and I get married too? Marco always said he wanted to be poly anyway."

"Okay, girl. Look, it's your life, and if you like it, I love it. I'm always gonna be team Zariah. So, I'm down for whatever you want to do."

"Thank you, Whisper. But I'm sure he gon' make this shit right. Now, let's stop talking about this shit. I'm trying to have fun, not stress myself out. Matter fact, I'm about to go to the bar and get us another round of drinks."

Zariah had just made her way to the bar when a tall man walked over to their table. Whisper looked up at the tall, dark-skinned man whose skin was as smooth as chocolate. He was dressed in Balmain from head to toe, and his Bad Bod cologne left a scent bubble around him.

"Is someone sitting here?" he asked, sitting down in the seat before Whisper could even respond.

"I'm actually here with my best friend. She just went to go get us some more drinks," Whisper replied, pointing over to Zariah at the bar.

"I didn't mean to intrude, but you are so beautiful. I had to at least come and introduce myself. My name is Truce," he announced, extending his hand.

"Nice to meet you, Truce. My name is Whisper." Whisper extended her hand and shook his.

"Can I buy you a drink, Whisper?"

"That's sweet, but no thank you. I'm just here, trying to have a good time with my best friend."

"Okay, I understand. I hope the two of you have a good

time. It was nice to meet you," Truce spoke before walking away from the table.

"Bitch, who the fuck was that? He was fine as hell," Zariah asked, walking back over to the table with their drinks in hand.

"I don't know, just some nigga that was trying to holla," Whisper revealed.

"Bitch, and you let his fine ass walk away? Did you get a good look at him? Cause from where I sit, that dude is like six foot three inches of fun. I would climb his ass like a fuckin' tree."

"Bitch, you crazy. I'm just trying to have a good time today. Plus, I'm way too involved in work right now for any male distractions. I don't have time for shit but making money. So, unless that nigga gonna give me a fifteen percent commission, I ain't got time for it."

Zariah and Whisper both laughed as they high fived each other. They spent the rest of the afternoon enjoying the day party, having drinks, and dancing to good music.

# CHAPTER TWO

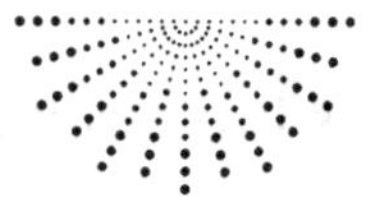

Tuesday morning came fast for Whisper. It seemed like she'd blinked her eyes and her three day weekend was over. She pulled into her office parking lot and walked into the building.

"Good morning, Whisper. Your coffee is already on your desk, and you have your first showing at eleven," Whisper's assistant, Ari, stated.

"Thank you, girl. You know how I be needing my morning coffee."

Whisper walked into her office and sat at her desk. It was nine-thirty, so that meant she had about an hour before she had to leave and head to the first house she was showing. She began answering emails, setting up two more house tours for that day. She could already tell that it would be a busy day, and she hoped that meant a lot of money was coming. Her phone rang, and she answered it quickly, seeing that it was Zariah.

"Hey, Z, what up doe?' Whisper answered cheerfully.

"Hey, girl, how you doing today? You workin' hard or hardly workin'?"

"I just got to the office about an hour ago, and I'm already about to go show a house. Then, I got two more after that."

"Oh, you getting to da money, and everybody mad," Zariah joked.

"Girl, you silly." Whisper laughed.

"I was calling to see if you wanted to meet at my restaurant for lunch today? I mean, I know you busy, but you still have to eat."

"I'm not sure about today, Z. I got so much work to do that it's crazy. I've been answering emails since I walked in, and they're still coming in. I just set up another showing for a house all the way in Sterling Heights while I've been on the phone with you. I'll probably just get something quick to eat. We can meet up sometime later in the week for lunch."

"Okay, that's cool. Call me when you get off," Zariah suggested before ending the call.

Moments later, Whisper was walking to her car and heading to her first location. When she pulled up to the three-bedroom, two-bathroom home a few miles from downtown Detroit, she saw that her client had yet to arrive. Walking inside the house, Whisper walked through every room, making sure nothing was out of place. She made sure she had every home staged before a showing so that her clients could get the full effect of the home. Moments later, she heard a car pull into the driveway, and she knew it was her client. Opening the door with a smile on her face, she saw a beautiful, brown-skinned woman with flowing curls walking up to the front door.

"Good morning, you must be Yara."

Yes, I am. It's nice to meet you," Yara spoke, extending her hand.

"It's nice to meet you as well. My name is Whisper, and I'll be showing you this home today. If you would follow me, we can get this tour started."

About forty-five minutes later, Yara was leaving the home, and Whisper was off to her next showing. The next house was a beautiful brick home in Farmington Hills that was worth one and a half million dollars. Whisper knew that selling this home would give her a very hefty commission. She'd not been at the home five minutes when a white Range Rover pulled up. Whisper smiled. She could tell from the car that pulled into the driveway that her next client had money. One thing Whisper absolutely hated was showing a home to someone who knew they couldn't afford it. It was a waste of her time.

She opened the door, and a huge smile spread across her face as the tall, dark-skinned man approached her.

"Truce, right?" Whisper asked, remembering him form the day party over the weekend.

"Whisper, second time this week. If I didn't know any

better, I would say this was a sign that we should be getting to know each other."

Whisper blushed, holding her head down as she smiled. Whisper had been single for so long that she'd gotten shy when men tried to talk to her. She liked her single life; however, she would be lying if she said she didn't miss the company of a man. Walking into the home, Whisper showed him every square inch of the home. At the end of the tour, Truce informed her that he would like to put in an offer. He then handed her a folder filled with all the necessary paperwork Whisper would need to put the offer in.

"That's wonderful. I'll put your offer in as soon as I get back to my office."

"Great, what happens next?" Truce asked.

"Well, once I put in the offer, we just have to wait for the owners to accept it. I know they will because the offer is the same as asking. After that, it usually takes several weeks before closing day."

"That's wonderful but not what I meant. What happens next with us? I feel like we should be going out to dinner or something."

"Truce, are you attempting to mix business with pleasure and asking me out on a date?" Whisper inquired.

"Only if you are saying yes. But if the answer is no then I didn't ask."

Whisper burst out into laughter. "You're funny, and I would love to go out to dinner with you."

Truce handed Whisper his cell phone, and she saved her

number in his contacts before calling herself so that she could have his number. He let her know he would be calling her later, so they could set something up. Smiling, Whisper agreed before walking Truce out of the house.

Around four that afternoon, Whisper finally walked back into her office. She had two offers to put in, and if they both were accepted, she would make over thirty thousand dollars in those two sales alone. She smiled, knowing this was about to be a great week for her. When she was done, Whisper shut down her computer, gathered her belongings, and headed home. Like clockwork, Mr. and Mrs. Johnston were sitting on their porch, sipping a glass of lemonade.

"Hi, Mr. and Mrs. Johnston. How y'all doing this evening?" Whisper called out.

"We're good, just out here enjoying this fresh air. How was work today? You always look good in them fancy suits you wear."

"Thank you, Mrs. Johnston. Work was good. I'm a little tired, so I'm just gonna chill for the rest of the night. Probably watch a movie or something. Y'all have a good night, and I'll see the both of you tomorrow."

Whisper made her way into her kitchen. She was hungry due to the fact that she'd skipped lunch and worked through it. Looking into her fridge, she didn't see anything that she wanted to eat, so she decided to Door Dash herself something. Picking a Middle Eastern restaurant not too far from her home, she ordered a charbroiled chicken dinner, making sure to order a large bowl of their garlic paste. Whisper wasn't really a picky eater; however, whenever she ate Middle Eastern food, she always had to have extra garlic paste. Once her order was placed, Whisper went to shower and change into her lounge clothes.

She'd just sat on her couch and turned her TV on when her phone rang. Looking down at the screen, she saw it was Truce, and she smiled, placing the phone to her ear as she answered.

"Hey, pretty lady, I hope I'm not interrupting anything," Truce spoke into the phone.

"Not at all. I'm just sitting here, scrolling Netflix, while I wait on my food," Whisper replied.

"Oh, okay. What you 'bout to eat?"

"I got something from this Middle Eastern spot not too far from my house."

"I love Middle Eastern food. But I can only eat it if the place has good garlic paste," Truce revealed.

"That's so funny. I'm the same way. The place I ordered from is called Beirut, and to me they have the best garlic paste."

"Really? I'ma have to try it out. Where is it?"

"It's in Romulus, not too far from the airport," Whisper uttered.

"Yeah, I'ma have to check that place out next time I'm in the area."

They spoke on the phone for about twenty more minutes until Whisper's order came. She enjoyed their conversation and couldn't wait to speak with Truce again. Whisper made her plate and turned on an episode of *Bridgerton*. She sat on the couch, watching a few more episodes, before she finally went to sleep.

The next morning, Whisper woke up to a "Good morning, Beautiful," text from Truce, and she couldn't help but smile. Making her way to her bathroom, she took a shower before searching her closet to find something to wear. She settled on a pair of red slacks and a short sleeved, white, button up shirt. Leaving the first three buttons unbuttoned, she tucked the shirt in before placing a gold Louis Vuitton necklace around her neck. She continued placing the matching set on her ears, wrist, and fingers before brushing her hair into a ponytail. Whisper flat ironed her bangs before placing wand curls into her ponytail. White Dior slingbacks graced her feet, and she knew she would have to sport the matching bag. After spraying herself with her scent of the day, she was ready for work.

Once Whisper arrived at the office, she went to her desk and immediately began answering emails. She set up a few more showings before opening an email that stated that the owners had accepted Truce's offer. *Damn, that was fast as hell. They must have really been ready to sell that house,* Whisper thought to herself as she replied to the email. Picking up her phone, she made the call to Truce.

"Damn, that was fast. What's the next step?" Truce asked, excited about the purchase of his new home.

"Well, next, you will put down a deposit. It's something we call earnest money. This is just to show the sellers that you are serious about the sale. If you want, you can meet me at the bank today, and we can set up your account to deposit the money in."

"Yeah, that's cool. What time works best for you?"

"How about eleven thirty? We can meet at the Chase bank on Ford Road in Garden City if that works for you," Whisper suggested.

"I'll see you there."

Whisper ended the call and went right back to answering emails. When she was done, she'd set up three more showings for later that afternoon. She prepared herself to go to the bank, leaving her office around eleven-fifteen. When she pulled into the parking lot, she didn't see Truce's Range Rover, so she called him.

"Hey, Truce, I'm here. How long before you get here?" Whisper asked.

"I'm here. I'm in this black BMW. I'm getting out the car now."

When Whisper spotted Truce's tall frame emerge from the car, she couldn't help but take a deep breath. He had on a pair of jeans and a Gucci t-shirt. His low cut Caesar blended well into his freshly trimmed goatee. *Damn, this man is fine,* she thought to herself, getting out of her car and walking over to him.

"Damn, pretty, is this how you step out at work?"

Just the sound of his beep baritone made her moist as she stared up into his beautiful brown eyes. Truce walked close to Whisper, towering over her. She was in a slight trance as she watched his muscular chest move with every breath he took.

"And you smell good too? What is that amazing smell?" Truce complimented.

"Thank you. It's Delina," Whisper revealed. "You ready to go start this account?" she continued.

Truce nodded his head, and the two of them walked into the bank together. When they were done, Whisper informed Truce that she had a few houses to show but would call him when she arrived home from work. Truce agreed before hugging Whisper and getting back into his car.

That night when Whisper arrived home, she spoke to Mr. and Mrs. Johnston the way she did every evening when she got home. But this time, there was no bubble bath. She quickly took a shower before putting on a pair of shorts and a tank top. When she was done, she placed a call to Truce, eager to talk to him.

"What up doe, my baby?" Truce answered.

"Hey, just got off work, just seeing what you were up to?" Whisper asked.

"Nothing much, just chillin'. You ate yet?"

"Nah, I haven't even seen what's in my fridge to cook yet."

"Get dressed and send me your address. I'm takin' you out to dinner."

It was something about the way he spoke that turned Whisper on. This was more like an order than an ask. She felt as though she didn't have an option to say no, and she didn't want to. She quickly rushed to her closet, picking out something to wear. She curled her hair and stepped into the black Chanel dress. She texted Truce her address before putting the finishing touches on her look. She'd just finished when her doorbell rang. Knowing it was Truce, she went downstairs and opened the door. Much to Whisper's surprise, Zariah stood on the other side.

"What you doing here, Z?" Whisper asked in confusion.

"Why you so dressed up on a Wednesday night?"

"I have a date if you must know. What are you doing here?" Whisper asked, stepping to the side so Zariah could enter.

"Bitch, what? Not queen single going on a date. Who you let get close enough to you to ask you out?"

"Shut up, Z. It's this guy I met, and he's gonna be here soon, so what's up?"

"You know what? Never mind. What I got to tell you can wait til tomorrow. I can't remember the last time I heard you say you were going on a date. Go knock the cobwebs off that pussy and call me tomorrow," Zariah joked before walking out the door.

Not too long after Zariah left, there was another knock at Whisper's door. Smiling, knowing it was indeed Truce, she opened the door. He stood there wearing an all-white Balmain ensemble. A gold Gucci link chain hung from around his neck, and a Rolex adorned his wrist. His Dior Sauvage cologne danced in Whisper's nose as she inhaled his scent. She loved a man that could match her fly in the fragrance department. She could tell that Truce was him.

"You ready to go, my baby?" Truce asked, holding out his hand to take Whisper's hand into his. She nodded her head yes before placing her hand gently into his. They walked out of her home, and Whisper closed and locked her door behind her.

"You look beautiful. I was gon' take you to Black Rock, but when you walked out in that, I felt like I needed to step my game up."

"Black Rock is fine with me if that's where you want to go. I like the way they cook the steak on stones," Whisper spoke.

Truce nodded his head and walked Whisper to his car. He opened her door and closed it once she got inside. Walking around the car, Truce smiled when he saw Whisper open his door for him from the inside. It was the same test he put every woman through. If she wouldn't have opened his door for him, Truce would have never talked to her again other than for business purposes. However, the fact that she'd opened the door let him know she was indeed a keeper.

Once they pulled up at the restaurant, they both got out the car, holding hands as they walked toward the door. Whisper felt good walking next to Truce, and she knew they looked good together as they walked through the door. They were seated quickly, and the waitress came to take their drink orders.

"What do you do for a living?" Whisper asked once the waitress walked away.

"I own a few laundromats around the city and a parking lot by the airport," Truce revealed. "My grandfather left me his laundromat when he passed, and I turned it into a chain. I used the money from those to buy the parking lot, and I been good ever since."

"Oh, an entrepreneur. I like that." Whisper smiled.

"Thanks, my baby. I appreciate that."

The two continued to get to know each other over dinner and a few more drinks. They were both having a wonderful time with one another, and neither of them wanted the night to end.

# CHAPTER THREE

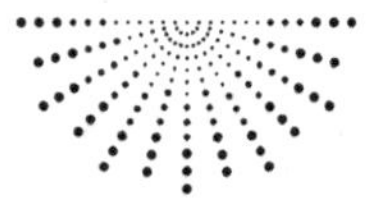

"*D*o you want to come inside?" Whisper asked once they made it back to her house.

Truce agreed, and Whisper led the way into her home. Truce took a seat on the couch, and Whisper asked him if he would like anything to drink, letting him know that she had water, juice, Tito's, or Hennessey.

"I'll take Hennessey," Truce requested. He watched Whisper walk to the kitchen, her round ass jiggling with each step. She returned several moments later with the bottle and two glasses.

"You wanna watch a movie or something?" Whisper suggested.

"Yeah, you turn on anything you want, and I'll watch it. It's whatever you wanna do," Truce spoke.

Whisper smiled and began scrolling through Hulu until

she found a movie that looked good. They sat on the couch, watching the movie, and Whisper curled up next to Truce, allowing him to cradle her in his arms. She laid her head on his strong chest, and Truce held her tighter. The embrace felt natural to both of them. Truce rubbed his hands over Whisper's soft body, and she closed her eyes. His touch was firm and strong, giving Whisper goosebumps as he ran his hands over her body.

Before Whisper knew it, they were kissing each other passionately. It had been a while since Whisper had sex, so she chose to take full advantage of the moment. She stood up slowly, taking Truce's hand into hers before leading him up into her bedroom. She continued to kiss his lips and neck.

"Whisper, are you sure you want to do this?" Truce questioned in a low tone. As much as he wanted Whisper in that moment, he didn't want to rush into anything. He liked Whisper, so he was willing to take his time with her.

"I'm sure that I want to feel you inside of me," Whisper replied seductively.

That was all Truce need to hear before he picked her up into his arms. Whisper wrapped her legs around Truce's waist, and she grabbed his face and kissed him. Truce placed her on the bed before sliding her panties off. Placing his head between her thighs, he savored her hungrily. Whisper's eyes rolled into the back of her head as Truce's tongue traced her clitoris. She moaned uncontrollably, holding his head in place as she grinded her hips slowly.

She was in pure ecstasy with each stroke of Truce's

tongue. "Does that feel good, my baby?" he whispered in-between licks.

"Yes, it feels so good," Whisper panted.

Coming up from between Whisper's legs, Truce began to undress. Whisper, following suit, removed her dress and bra, standing in front of Truce fully naked. He removed his pants and boxers, exposing his erect manhood, catching Whisper off guard by the size. His nine-inch manhood stood so thick that Whisper salivated by his meatiness. Walking closer to him, she pushed Truce onto her bed, dropping to her knees. Using both hands, she leaned onto the bed and took him into her mouth. Whisper used every jaw muscle she had to ensure she made him feel the same way he'd just made her feel.

"Damn, baby, do that shit. Suck that dick," Truce moaned as Whisper used one of her hands and began cuffing his balls.

Truce curled his toes as he felt Whisper's warm, wet mouth around his manhood. He'd never been sucked like this before, and if he wasn't careful, he would be telling Whisper he loved her soon. Pulling himself from her mouth, Truce stood to his feet. Reaching for his pants, he pulled out a condom before placing it onto his shaft. Whisper licked her lips as she anticipated what was to come. Truce climbed on top of her and eased himself into her, both of them moaning upon entry. Whisper gripped him tightly as he pumped in and out of her.

"Shit, where the fuck have you been all my life?" Truce whispered into her ear before looking into her eyes.

The lust was so passionate that Truce thought he was going to nut through the condom and get her pregnant. Her walls were so tight that it felt as though Truce would bust with each thrust. *Damn, how the fuck pussy this good just fall into my lap?* he thought to himself as he tongue kissed Whisper.

Wrapping her legs around his waist, Whisper flipped Truce over, placing herself on top. She rode him to her own rhythm as Truce grabbed her plump ass.

"Shit, baby, this pussy so good. This shit gon' make a nigga nut."

"Don't cum yet, Daddy. Hold it in so we can cum together," Whisper spoke, closing her eyes and picking up her speed. When Truce grabbed her firm breasts and began twirling her nipples between his fingers, she could no longer hold it.

"Shit, I'm 'bout to cum. You gon' cum with me, Daddy?" Whisper encouraged.

"Hell yeah, this pussy making that dick cum, my baby."

Once they were finished, Whisper laid on Truce's chest, spent. Both of them were in awe at how good the sex had been between them. Whisper felt herself becoming sleepy and knew that she would need a shower before bed.

"I'm not trying to put you out or nothing, but I gotta get up for work in the morning," Whisper said, raising up from Truce's chest.

"Damn, my baby. You just gon' fuck me like that and put me out? That's how you get down?"

"It's not like that, Truce. It's just after midnight, and I still have to take a shower. Believe me, if I didn't have to work in the morning, you could stay for round two."

"It's all good. Maybe I'll take you up on that this weekend."

Truce got up from the bed and dressed before Whisper walked him to the door. He hugged her tightly, kissing her on her neck before walking out the door. Truce thought about the way Whisper's pussy felt his entire ride home, anticipating the next time they saw each other. He'd never had a woman tell him to leave before, and the fact that Whisper had done just that only made him want her more.

THE NEXT MORNING, WHISPER WOKE UP TO A "GOOD morning, Beautiful" text from Truce. However, she didn't text back until after she got to her office. Honestly, Truce was giving Whisper butterflies, and she didn't know how to feel about that. She'd just pressed send on her phone when her assistant walked inside her office with a bouquet of red and white roses.

"Girl, these just came for you. Let me find out you finally letting somebody get close to you," Ari joked, handing Whisper the flowers.

Smiling, Whisper read the note, and it was indeed from Truce. Picking up her phone, she sent a text to Truce, thanking him for the flowers. He immediately called her, letting her know that he needed to see her again. Truthfully, Truce hadn't gotten Whisper off his mind since last night.

"Can we chill and watch a movie tonight? I'll bring some takeout too," Truce suggested.

"Yeah, that would be cool. I'll hit you up when I get off."

"Cool, talk to you later, my baby," Truce spoke before ending the call.

Whisper went on about her day, making her way to the one showing she had scheduled that morning. During the showing, Whisper received a call from Zariah. She had forgotten to call her after her date with Truce. *I'ma call her as soon as I leave this showing,* Whisper thought to herself, silencing her phone before placing it back into her purse. She finished showing the house then made her way back to the office to put in the offer her clients had made. Once she was finished, she was finally able to return Zariah's call.

"Damn, bitch, I thought that nigga had kidnapped you or something. I was gonna be at yo house tonight if you didn't call me back," Zariah announced as soon as she picked up the phone.

"My bad, girl. My date didn't end til really late last night, and I been a little busy at work today."

"Oh, shit, you gave that nigga some pussy, didn't you?" Zariah laughed.

"Now what would make you say that? When have you ever known me to give up my pussy on the very first date? I mean, I did, but I'm asking what made you think that?"

Zariah burst out into laughter. She knew her friend all

too well. "Girl, you must really like this man. Who the hell is he?" Zariah asked.

"You remember that guy that I met at the day party?"

"You mean that fine ass, tall ass, chocolate specimen that you tried to act like you didn't want to talk to?"

"Well, I didn't at the party. I was just chillin' with you. But I ended up showing him a house a couple days later. He took me out last night to celebrate his offer being accepted," Whisper revealed.

"Okay. So, bitch, how was it?" Zariah asked.

"Girl, the sex was wonderful. I can't remember the last time I had Vitamin D that strong. But it's not just the sex. I like him. And we look so good together. And did I mention that man smells amazing? He sent flowers to my office this morning, and he's bringing dinner over tonight."

"Girl, you 'bout to have a whole man. It's about damn time," Zariah joked. "On some real shit though, sis, I'm happy for you. You deserve this shit," she continued.

"We all deserve to be happy, Zariah. And speaking of that, what did you want to tell me last night?"

"Girl, we can talk about that later. I'm too happy for you to ruin this moment with shit about my crazy ass relationship."

"Oh, hell no. Don't do that. Whatever it was had you at my door, so you might as well tell me what's up, Z."

Zariah took a deep breath before responding. "I'm pregnant," she revealed.

Whisper sat there for a moment with her mouth wide

open. She didn't know what to say. Her best friend was telling her that she was pregnant with a married man's baby. Her heart instantly went out to her friend because she knew this was not going to work out in her favor. She just hoped Zariah knew.

"Oh, my God, Z. What did Marco say?" Whisper asked.

"He doesn't know yet. He's out of town, and I don't want to tell him over the phone."

"Yeah, I get that. How do you feel about it?"

"Honestly, Whisper, I would love to have that man's baby. It's something that we've always talked about. I love him, Whisper, and this baby would be proof of our love."

"Zariah, you do realize that you're talkin' 'bout a married man, right? A man that literally chose another woman over you. Why do you even want him, Z? You are a dope ass woman that can do so much better."

"Whisper, I didn't tell you so that you can judge me. I am fully aware that Marco is married. I feel the pain of that shit every day. Look, I'ma just talk to you another time."

Before Whisper could say another word, Zariah hung up. Whisper hated to see her friend so hurt. By no means was she trying to place any judgement on her best friend. She just wanted her to know that she was worthy of real love, and Marco was not the one that was going to give her that. Whisper thought about calling Zariah back but quickly decided against it, wanting to give her time to cool off.

# CHAPTER FOUR

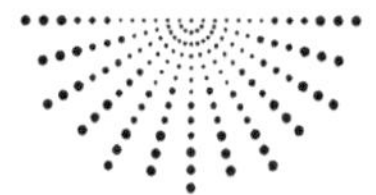

$\mathcal{I}$t had been a few weeks, and Whisper and Truce had been together every day. Whisper enjoyed Truce's company and was eager to see him every day. It was closing day for him, and they'd planned a celebratory dinner later that night. Truce walked into the office, looking fine as hell in a black Armani suit. The black Armani button up he had under his suit jacket had the first three buttons undone, giving a glimpse of his muscular chest. Truce walked into Whisper's office and took a seat.

"What up doe, my baby? You got a nigga excited 'bout today," Truce spoke.

"You should be excited. The purchase of a house is a huge milestone in anyone's life. I'm very proud of you, baby. And that big ass commission check was an added bonus."

"Yeah, I know that shit made them pockets phat. I think you need to be taking me out tonight," Truce joked.

"I got you, Dada. Be ready by seven tonight." Whisper smiled, placing the paperwork she needed him to sign in front of him. "Sign the necessary places and the keys are yours," Whisper continued.

Truce signed on every line before standing to his feet, pulling Whisper closer to him. He kissed her as he grabbed a handful of her ass. "I want to fuck you so bad," he whispered into her ear, placing his hand under her skirt and finding her wetness. He inserted two fingers inside her, and she moaned out loud. *Damn, even this man's fingers feel good.*

Truce kissed Whisper's neck as he fingered her to an orgasm right there in her office. "This is just a preview of what you have to look forward to when you get off work tonight. Keep my pussy ready, my baby." Truce kissed Whisper's lips before walking out of her office.

She rushed to her door, closing it before walking over to her desk. She took a pack of baby wipes from the drawer and began cleaning herself up. Truce made her want to take an early day and go home right then. Just thinking about his dick inside of her almost made her cum for a second time.

"Girl, who the fuck was that fine ass man?" Ari asked, walking into Whisper's office as soon as she opened the door.

"That's my man."

"Oh, so that's the guy that's been sending flowers to this

office for you. Girl, that man is so fine. Does he have a brother?"

"I know he fine, and nah, he's the only child," Whisper revealed.

WHEN WHISPER ARRIVED HOME AFTER WORK, SHE CALLED Truce and let him know she was home. She was going to take him out to dinner, but instead, she chose to cook for him. So, as soon as she'd gotten off, she made a quick stop at the grocery store, picking up everything she needed for her famous Tuscan salmon pasta. She had about an hour and a half before Truce got there. Heading into her kitchen, she poured herself a glass of wine before turning on her Bluetooth. *Best Part* by HER bumped through the small speaker as she began to cook.

Once everything was done, she quickly went into her bathroom to take a shower. She picked out a light pink, two-piece outfit before choosing her perfume. She sprayed Valentino's Donna Born in Roma all over her body. She'd just finished when Truce texted her, letting her know he was outside. Making her way down the stairs, she opened the door and let Truce inside.

"What's up, my baby?" Truce greeted as he embraced Whisper.

"I was gonna take you out to dinner tonight, but I decided to cook for you instead. We went out to eat every night this week, so I think it's time for a home cooked meal."

"Damn, my baby, you cooked for me? I feel special now," Truce joked.

"You are special."

Whisper took Truce's hand and led him into the kitchen. He took a seat at the table, and Whisper began to make his plate. It was rare that Whisper cooked for any man, but Truce made her want to be different for him. Bringing his plate to the table, she set it in front of him before pouring him a glass of wine.

"Damn, this shit looks good, baby," Truce complimented.

Once Whisper made her plate and sat at the table, they both began to eat. She smiled seeing Truce clean his plate, knowing he'd enjoyed the food. Whisper finished her wine before pouring herself another glass.

"Damn, that shit was good as hell. Thank you for cookin', baby."

"You're welcome. This was just something quick. I really be getting down in the kitchen."

"Oh, okay. I'ma need to taste everything."

"I got you, baby." Whisper smiled.

"What you doing this weekend?" Truce asked, looking into Whisper's eyes.

"I don't have nothing planned. You got something you wanna do?"

"Yeah, I was thinkin' we should go to Miami for the weekend. We could fly out Friday morning and come back Monday," Truce suggested.

Whisper's face lit up as she jumped up to hug Truce. A

vacation was just what she needed, so she was more than happy with Truce's suggestion.

"I'll take that as a yes." Truce laughed as he hugged Whisper back tightly.

"Oh, I can't wait. You don't know how bad I need a damn vacation. It's been a couple of years since I took one. Thank you, baby."

Truce reached into his pocket and pulled out a wad of blue faced bills. Splitting the stack, he handed half of it to Whisper.

"What's this for?" she asked, confused.

"Take the day off work tomorrow and go get everything you need for the trip. I'm gon' book the flights tonight. You wanna stay in a hotel or an Airbnb?"

"Whichever you choose is fine with me," Whisper spoke without giving it a second thought.

Truce nodded his head before standing from his seat and grabbing the dinner plates.

"What you doing, baby?" Whisper asked, perplexed.

"I'm about to wash the dishes. You cooked, so it's only right that I clean up after."

*Damn, this man is literally everything. He gon' take me on a trip and clean my kitchen? Yeah, I ain't never getting off him.* When Truce was done washing the dishes, they made their way up to Whisper's room. They made love that night. The lust was gone, and love had entered. Although it was unspoken, they both felt it.

. . .

TRUCE WAS AT WHISPER'S HOUSE BRIGHT AND EARLY FRIDAY morning. He helped her with the luggage she'd packed and put them into the trunk of his car. One would think they were going for weeks instead of a weekend by the two huge suitcases full of items that Whisper packed. They had unknowingly matched, wearing a pair of black Balenciaga joggers, a white shirt, and a matching Balenciaga fitted cap.

"Damn, you was in my closet this morning or something?" Whisper joked.

"I guess great minds just think alike. Let's take a picture," Truce suggested.

Whisper agreed, standing in front of Truce as they cuddled up for a selfie. Truce kissed Whisper on her cheek, and he snapped another picture.

"Now don't y'all look cute," Mrs. Johnston called out from across the street.

"Thank you." Whisper blushed. "Mrs. Johnston, this is Truce. Truce, this is Mrs. Johnston," she introduced.

"It's nice to meet you, Mrs. Johnston." Truce waved.

"It's nice to meet you too, baby. You sholl is fine."

"Mrs. Johnston!" Whisper laughed.

"What? I'm old not blind. That's a fine ass man right there. I hope you know what to do with him. If not, come on over and I'll tell you some tricks."

"No, thank you. We're actually on our way to the airport. We don't want to miss our flight, so we gotta hurry. I'll see you when I get back, Mrs. Johnston," Whisper spoke as she rushed inside the car. The conversation was getting a little too awkward for her, so she had to end it.

"That little old lady got some freak in her," Truce joked as he pulled out of Whisper's driveway.

When they landed in Miami, Truce requested an Uber to pick them up from the airport. The resort they were staying on had everything, so there was no need for them to rent a car. After checking into their room, they both went straight to the shower, washing the flight off.

"What you want to do first?" Truce asked, going through the brochures.

"Let's go get some massages," Whisper suggested.

Truce agreed, liking Whisper's suggestion. After they were dressed, they went down to the spa and got an hour-long couple's massage.

Once they were back in their room, they dressed for the night before going to one of the five restaurants the resort offered. Once they were done eating, they went to the casino. They had fun their first night in Miami and ended it making love in their room to a view of the city lights.

Their weekend in Miami ended rather quickly, and it was bittersweet for Whisper as they made their way back to the airport. It was back to work the very next day, and Whisper wished she'd taken a longer vacation. Truce promised her that they would take another vacation soon, so at least she had that to look forward to.

When they pulled back up to Whisper's house, he helped her with her luggage before kissing her on her forehead.

"You not stayin', babe?" Whisper asked.

"Nah, I gotta go check on a few things. I might be back later tonight though. If not, then I'll definitely be back tomorrow," Truce informed.

"Okay, baby. Call me later and be safe." Whisper kissed Truce before watching him walk to his car and drive away. He'd just left, and Whisper missed him already. She didn't know how she'd gotten so deep in so quickly. However, she knew there was only one way to describe the way she way feeling about Truce, and that was love.

TRUCE WALKED INTO HIS CONDO AND LOOKED AT THE SEVERAL moving boxes that were throughout his living room. Because he'd taken Whisper to Miami, he didn't move over the weekend like he'd planned. So, he knew today had to be the day.

"Hey, baby, how was your trip?" Truce's wife, Yara, asked, greeting her husband at the door.

"It was just business, baby. I met with a few people, shook a few hands. You know how that shit goes. I couldn't wait to get back to you and move us into our dream home," Truce lied. The truth was he'd had a great time with Whisper, and he would have rather stayed in Miami with her a few days longer. However, he didn't want the drama that would have come with that. Yara was more than ready to move, and

Truce would have never heard the end of it if he would have prolonged it even more.

"I missed you, baby," Yara cooed, wrapping her arms around her husband and kissing him passionately.

"I missed you too, boo. What you do while I was gone?"

"Nothing, just finished up the rest of the packing. Everything is boxed up and ready to be put in the U-Haul."

"See, that's why you my baby. You always on yo shit," Truce complimented. "I'm about to go rent the truck. I'll be back in a few. Tonight, we gonna make love in every room in our new house," he continued.

"Then you need to hurry up and move this stuff, so we can get to it. I'm ready to show you how much I missed you."

"Okay, I was gonna Uber up there, but why don't you just drop me off? That's probably gonna be quicker. I'm trying to hurry up and get in that pussy tonight," Truce suggested.

Yara took Truce to U-Haul and followed him back to their condo once the truck was rented. Truce could have hired movers; however, he didn't like just anyone in his home or around his things. So, he decided he would move everything himself. Yara had indeed made it easier for him, packing everything in boxes. They began loading the truck as soon as they got back. Once the truck was full and had no room left to put anything else inside, they dropped their first load of items off.

"Baby, I can't believe how big this house is. When you told me you put an offer in for it without me seeing it first, I was a little skeptical. But baby, this is beautiful. It's much nicer than any of the houses I saw. I can't wait to decorate it and put my touches on it. It's gonna be so nice," Yara gushed.

"I know you're going to make this house a beautiful home for us. I can't wait to fill this home with babies we made," Truce continued, hugging his wife and kissing her on the forehead.

Truce and Yara had been together for five years and had been married for the last two. He loved Yara with all of his heart. She was the most loyal person Truce had ever met. That was the reason he married her. When he first met her, Truce thought Yara was the most beautiful woman he'd ever seen. She stood five foot six inches tall with smooth caramel skin. She stayed in the gym the same way Truce did, and she had a body most women would pay for. Not to mention, she was a hustler. Yara owned an online candle company that brought in a nice amount of money each year. She also had started being active on TikTok. Although he didn't have a huge following like some of the other TikTokers, she was able to bring in a couple hundred dollars a month from it.

With all the money Truce made, Yara didn't have to work, and she knew that. However, she chose to work every day, making sure she would always have her own money to spend. She was the woman of every hood nigga's dream, and she was Truce's reality. Although Truce had done his dirt, cheating on Yara a time or two, she'd never found out. That was mainly because Truce had never taken it any further than sex. However, with Whisper, it was different. Whisper was the first woman other than Yara that Truce could see himself giving his heart to.

They made it back to their condo, ready to load the truck for a second time. Yara walked into the house to grab more boxes, giving Truce enough time to shoot a quick text to Whisper. He let her know that he wouldn't be able to make it back to see her but would definitely come tomorrow. Once he saw Whisper's response, he put his phone back into his packet before Yara walked back outside.

By nine that night, they had finished moving everything, and Truce was putting together their bed. Yara got into the shower, and once Truce was done, he joined her, pulling her close to him as the water from their rain shower ran down their bodies. Yara grabbed a towel and the soap before washing Truce's body, cleaning him from top to bottom. She allowed the soap to rinse clean before dropping to her knees and taking him into her mouth.

"Damn, baby, that shit feels good," Truce panted as his eyes rolled to the back of his head.

Yara sucked her husband until he released himself into her mouth. Once out of the shower, they made their way into the master bedroom. Truce laid on their king-sized bed and motioned Yara over to him. She obliged, straddling his face as his tongue danced around her wetness. Yara moaned aloud as she grabbed her breasts, twirling her nipples between her fingers. She slowly grinded on his face as he savored her sweet nectar.

"I want to feel you inside of me," Yara moaned softly,

sliding down from his face to his manhood and easing down on top of him. Truce moaned as he entered her. She was so wet, and Truce could tell that his wife missed him.

"Damn, baby, this pussy so wet," Truce moaned.

"It's only for you, Daddy," Yara whispered. With those words, Truce lost control, reaching his climax quicker than expected, releasing himself inside of Yara.

Yara made her way into the bathroom, washing herself before bringing a towel to Truce. They lay in bed, spent, as they drifted off to sleep.

WHISPER SAT AT THE TABLE ACROSS FROM ZARIAH AS THEY ATE lunch. Whisper hadn't spoken with her since before she went to Miami. So, she knew they had a lot of catching up to do.

"So, how was your trip? Did you have a good time?" Zariah asked before popping a fry into her mouth.

"It was wonderful. We had so much fun. I can't wait for our next vacation."

"Damn, you really like this man, huh? Are y'all getting serious?"

"Yeah, I'm pretty sure I love him. I know we been moving kinda fast, but it's all so natural, and I didn't expect that. Truce just makes me feel different."

"And I love that for you." Zariah smiled.

"Enough about me, what's up with you and Marco? Have you told him you were pregnant yet?"

"Yeah, I told him," Zariah responded, dropping her head low.

"Okay, and what happened?"

Whisper saw the tears as they formed in Zariah's eyes. Her heart instantly went out to her friend, knowing she was hurt by the outcome. Reaching over the table, Whisper rubbed Zariah's hand, letting her know that everything would be okay.

"He wants me to have an abortion. He said he can't have any children outside of his marriage. Like what the fuck, Whisper? He's been fuckin' me for years, and now me and my baby are outsiders? He was with me first." Zariah's voice cracked as tears ran down her face. "That muthafucka acts like he don't even care about me. Like I didn't come first. He says he married her for their daughter, but I'm having his child too. I bet he didn't ask her to get a fuckin' abortion when she told him she was pregnant. He wasn't scared to have no outside babies on me. Oh, but he don't want to hurt her," Zariah continued.

"Z, that's his wife. What do you want him to do? He don't want to lose his family, and I know it's fucked up, and he ain't shit for this. But in reality, he picked her over you when he married her. So, he's damn sure going to pick that family over the child you're carrying. Why even put yourself or that baby through that?" Whisper questioned.

"What you saying, Whisper? You agree with him? I should have an abortion?"

"No, that's not what I'm saying at all. That is your body,

so nobody can tell you what to do with it. What I am saying is that if you choose to have the baby, just know you're going to be raising it by yourself. He's not going to be there. He's going to lie and break promises the same way he's doing now. Only this time, it will be you and that baby he's doing it to."

Zariah nodded her head, knowing that what Whisper was saying was true. Although she couldn't see herself killing her baby, she didn't know if she wanted to be a single mother either. She had a lot going on with her restaurants and the staff. She already didn't think there was enough time in a day to do everything. So, she knew by adding a baby to the equation, everything would be twice as hard. She would have to do a lot of thinking and not make any rash decisions.

After lunch, Whisper went back to her office. She had two offers that she needed to put in before the end of the day. If accepted, both homes would bring in six figures in combined commission. Whisper was at her desk when Ari walked inside her office.

"Hey, girl, a lady came by looking for you while you were at lunch. She didn't want to work with any of the other agents, and she wouldn't leave her name. She just said she would come back later," Ari informed.

"Oh, okay. I guess I'll just wait for her to come back. Once I finish with this, I'm going to be going home. So, if you want to leave early today, it's fine with me," Whisper suggested.

"Will I still get paid for the whole day? Because if not, I'll just stay."

"I got you, girl. Go enjoy some of this beautiful day. I know damn well you don't want to be stuck inside this office."

"Thanks, girl." Ari beamed, rushing out of Whisper's office and grabbing her things. "I'll see you tomorrow. And thanks again, girl," Ari called out before walking out the door.

Whisper finished the rest of her work before making her way home. When she pulled into her driveway, Mrs. Johnston called her, motioning Whisper to come across the street.

"Hey, Mrs. Johnston. How are you doing today?" Whisper asked as she walked onto the porch.

"I'm good, baby. I just wanted to let you know that some woman came to your house today. I've never seen her before, but she knocked for a while before I finally told her no one was home. I don't know who she was, but she was a younger girl, around your age, and she drove a white car."

"A white car?" Whisper asked, perplexed. "I don't know who that was. Whoever it was must not be too important because they don't have my number to call me. Thank you for the information, Mrs. Johnston."

Whisper walked back across the street and into her house. She went right up to her bathroom, the same why she did every day when she got off, and ran herself a bath. Before she got inside, Truce texted her, telling her he was on his way over. Whisper told him she was about to take a bath but would leave the door unlocked for him. Once she finally got into the tub, she turned on her music and began to soak.

"Hey, baby, how was your day at work?" Truce asked once he entered the bathroom.

"It was cool. I put in two offers today."

"That's right, baby, get that money."

"You wanna go out for dinner tonight, or you wanna order in?" Whisper asked.

"It's whatever you want, baby. This yo world."

Whisper smiled. She loved the way Truce treated her like a queen. She opted to stay in and order food, and Truce was more than okay with that. They both decided on Indian food, and Truce placed the order. By the time their food got there, Whisper was out of the tub and scrolling Netflix, looking for something to watch. Truce made their plates before bringing them into the living room and handing one to Whisper.

"Have you ever watched *Your Honor*? They just put it on Netflix, and everyone been saying it's good. We can check it out," Whisper suggested.

"Yeah, let's check it out."

Whisper pressed play, and they began watching the show. The show was so good that they couldn't stop watching. They watched four episodes before turning it off. Yara had been calling Truce for the past two hours, and he was happy he'd put his phone on silent. Although he didn't want an argument with his wife, he didn't want to explain to Whisper that he had a wife. He didn't want to lose Whisper, and he thought telling her the truth would do just that.

"You got an early day tomorrow?" Truce asked.

"Not too early. Why? What's up?"

"Let's go upstairs and I'll show you what's up."

Whisper smiled and followed Truce up to her room. He knew Yara was already mad so staying out a little later wouldn't make that big of a difference. Pulling Whisper toward him, he kissed her passionately before pulling her shirt over her head, exposing her bare breasts. He took one into his mouth, sucking on it tenderly.

"I want to make love to you, baby. I don't want us to have sex anymore," Truce whispered.

"Baby, are you saying…"

"Yes, I'm saying I love you. And I want us to be together officially as a couple."

"Really? You want to be with me?"

"Hell yeah, I gotta put claim to this. I don't ever want to lose you," Truce confirmed.

"You ain't never gon' lose me, baby. I love you too," Whisper revealed. "So, this means you my man now?"

"Always yo man, baby," Truce replied.

Whisper smiled, and just like her man said, they made love all through the night. Truce was so tired after their love making that he fell asleep right there in Whisper's bed, not going home to the wife that was waiting for him.

# CHAPTER FIVE

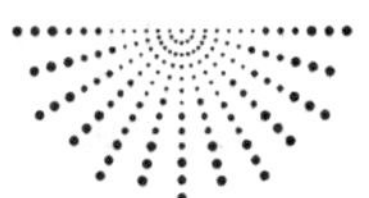

When Whisper's clock alarmed at seven that morning, she rolled over to see Truce sleeping peacefully. Not wanting to wake him, she slowly got out of bed and headed to her bathroom. Once out of the shower, she headed back into her room to see that Truce was now awake and getting dressed.

"My bad, baby. Did I wake you when I got out of bed?" she asked.

"Nah, you good. I needed to get up anyway. I gotta go check on my parking lot and make sure all the hotels in the area have enough parking vouchers for the week."

"You coming back tonight?"

"I'm not sure yet, but I will call and let you know. And we definitely going to the drive in this weekend to see that movie you wanted to see," Truce revealed.

"Okay, baby."

"I love you, and I'll call you later," Truce spoke before kissing Whisper and walking out the door.

Whisper walked into her office smiling from ear to ear. Truce had come into her life and warmed her entire heart. This was the first time in a long time that Whisper had truly been happy with another person. She'd had relationships in the past. However, none had amounted to the love that she felt for Truce. She didn't understand how she had such strong feelings so quickly, but she did.

"Oh, here, she is walking in right now." Whisper heard Ari say. "Whisper, this is the client I told you about yesterday." Ari pointed, getting Whisper's attention.

"Hello, I'm sorry, I'm just walking in. If you would like to follow me into my office, we can speak there," Whisper said, still smiling. She led the woman to her office, closing her door before placing her briefcase on her desk. "The fact that you're showing up to my office is crazy. And I know that was you that came to my house yesterday. You can't do that shit. I told you I would call you when I had some information for you. And I haven't called you yet, so what the fuck are you doing?" Whisper chastised, still trying to keep her tone low.

"I gave you a down payment of five thousand dollars a month ago, and all you have told me was that my husband was cheating. I haven't received any pictures or anything. You came highly recommend by a friend of mine, and she told me all about your work. Why is it taking you so long?"

"Listen, Yara, this is a process, and I am very thorough. I

want to be sure I have all the information. I can confirm the cheating, but I can't confirm how far he wants to take the cheating," Whisper revealed.

"Was he with you all night?" Yara asked.

"Yes, he was."

"So, you are fucking my husband, huh?"

"Yes, that's exactly what you're paying me for, correct?" Whisper questioned.

"Yes, it is, but I need pictures. Like I stated before, we have a prenuptial agreement, so I have to have proof of his cheating for anything to stand," Yara informed.

"Yes, I understand. Just give me a week and I will have some pictures for you."

Whisper had indeed taken on Yara as a client the day she'd came to one of her showings. Being a realtor made her six figures. However, helping women catch their cheating mates was priceless. Even though it paid very well, she didn't do it for the money. She knew how horrible men could be. They would have a wonderful life with a loving wife and children, and they would still fuck it up for a big ass and a pretty face. She'd done this for years, selling her services on the black market.

Whisper had been able to go on dates and sleep with men without catching any feelings just to assure the wives received the information they needed. However, things were different with Truce. Whisper had fallen in love with him. Although it was something she didn't mean to happen, she welcomed the feeling. Whisper hated that she'd found love under these circumstances; however, this was reality.

"Okay, Whisper, one week and then I'ma need those pictures. I'll talk to you then," Yara agreed before walking out the door.

"Fuck, what the hell did I get myself into?" Whisper said aloud to herself as she took a seat at her desk. She didn't want to lose Truce, and she knew that if she told him the truth, he would leave her. She also knew once she gave Yara the pictures she wanted and she confronted Truce with them, he would leave her. She had to figure out a way to get Yara what she wanted and still keep Truce.

Despite what Whisper had going on, she still worked her main job like the professional she was, showing houses and putting in offers left and right. Once her workday was over, she made her way home with Truce heavy on her mind. Whisper called him as soon as she got into the house and became a bit uneasy when he didn't answer. She walked into her bathroom, taking her evening bath before calling him back. When Truce didn't answer for a second time, she immediately became nervous. There had never been a time that she called him that he didn't answer, and she had no clue what was going on.

*What if Yara told him? What if he knows she hired me to spy on him? Why the fuck ain't he answering?* So many thoughts were running through her head, and she didn't know which one to listen to. Making her way down to her kitchen,

Whisper poured herself a glass of wine, not knowing what to do next.

"Baby, I'm sorry. I told you I had to make an unexpected trip to Cleveland. Yara, you know me. So, you know if it's money on the floor, I'm going. I ain't letting no money pass me up. When you were calling me, I was in a meeting with the owners of the nightclub I want to buy. By the time I got out the meeting, my phone had died, and my car charger was broken. It was late as fuck, so I just got a room because I was too tired to drive all the way back. I got into the room and thought I had my charger with me and didn't. I was too tired to do anything else but sleep, so that's what I did. I woke up and drove back home as soon as I could," Truce lied.

"Why didn't you call me from the room?" Yara asked.

"I tried, but the front desk told me they restricted all calls from the room due to outsiders calling and scamming their guests."

Truce had an answer for everything, but Yara already knew the truth. It hurt her heart that her husband would lie to her. However, she knew exactly where her husband had been. She also knew everything that was coming out of his mouth was a lie. Instead of continuing to make a big deal about it, she just said okay, sweeping everything under the rug. Yara was playing chess, not checkers, so she knew she would have the last laugh.

"You wanna go out to dinner tonight?" Truce asked, knowing he would have to put in major work.

"Yeah, I do. See if you can make us reservations at The Whitney for tonight," Yara suggested.

Truce nodded his head and went to go make the reservation. Yara headed upstairs to their bedroom. She knew she had packed a copy of their prenuptial agreement in the box with all the rest of their important papers, and she wanted to read over it again. She'd only saw it once when she signed it, and that had been years ago. Taking the box into her closet and closing the door, Yara quickly thumbed through the papers until she found what she was looking for. She placed the papers inside one of the many purses she had on display inside the closet before taking the box back inside the bedroom.

"I was able to make us reservations for seven tonight," Truce informed as he walked into the room.

"Okay, cool. I'm about to start gettin' dressed," Yara uttered before heading into the bathroom.

Truce knew Yara would be inside the bathroom for quite a while, so he decided to use that time to call Whisper. There was no way he would be able to go back to Whisper's house that night. He knew he was on thin ice with Yara, and he didn't need anything breaking it. Calling Whisper, he made up a lie about him having food poisoning from a sub he had for lunch. When Whisper asked if he needed her to come over and bring him anything, he quickly told her no, letting her know that he just needed to stay in bed and drink a lot of fluids to flush his system. Whisper agreed, and Truce told her he should be feeling better by the weekend, and they could go out. Yara and Truce spent the rest of their evening together, truly enjoying the other's company.

W HISPER SAT AT HER DESK THE NEXT MORNING, MIND RACING. Yara wanted pictures; however, she knew she couldn't be the one to take them. If Yara showed them to Truce, he would know for sure that it was her that had taken them. *He would never forgive me. I want a life with this man. How the fuck can I set him up?* After several moments of contemplation, Whisper finally came up with a plan she thought could work. Picking up her phone, she made a call to Zariah.

"Hey, girl, what's up?" Zariah answered.

"Where you at, Z? I need your help."

"I'm at my restaurant, the one in Southfield. You good?"

"I'm on my way," Whisper voiced before ending the call.

Whisper walked out of her office, letting Ari know she was going out for lunch. When Whisper walked into Seafood and Soul, the hostess sat her at the table immediately, and Whisper texted Zariah, letting her know she was there. A short time later, Zariah was joining her at the table.

"Whisper, what's wrong?" Zariah asked, taking a seat at the table.

"Girl, I need a favor. And I know this might be a lot for me to ask, but I just don't see any other way."

"Whisper, what is it? Is everything okay?" Zariah looked

at her best friend and saw the uneasy look in her eyes. She seemed unhinged, and Zariah wanted desperately to know what it was about.

"Z, I need you to follow me on a date and take pictures of us."

"Bitch, you need me to do what?" Zariah laughed, not understanding what was going on.

"Believe me, I know it sounds crazy, but I wouldn't be asking if this wasn't important. The less you know the better, but please do this for me, Z."

With those words, Zariah agreed to help her friend. She never liked involving outside people in her side hustle, and not even her best friend knew what she did. However, if she didn't want to lose Truce, she knew she would have to do things she'd never done. She informed Zariah she would let her know the day and time before thanking her. Whisper stayed and talked with Zariah for a moment before leaving and heading back to her office. Whisper felt like a weight had been lifted from her, and she was able to continue work as normal for the rest of the day.

When Whisper arrived home, she placed a call to Truce. He hadn't so much as texted her all day, and that was unlike him. Truce answered her call on the second ring, and the sound of his voice calmed her soul. They talked for a moment with Truce letting her know that he would see her tomorrow. Whisper happily agreed before ending the call.

· · ·

IT WAS TEN O'CLOCK ON A FRIDAY MORNING, AND IT WAS already eighty degrees in the city. The sun beamed down on Yara as she made her way to her car. She'd made an appointment with a lawyer to read over her prenuptial agreement, and she was eager to know the outcome. She loved her husband with all of her heart, but she refused to get played. The prenuptial agreement Truce had asked her to sign never meant anything to her. In her mind, she was marrying her soulmate, and they would be together forever. However, Truce had broken their vows and broken her trust.

Yara walked into her lawyer's office and took a seat at his desk. Attorney Nathan Blackwell was one of the best in the city. Yara knew that if anyone could help her, he would be the one to do it.

"Mrs. Washington, I'm glad you could meet me today. I've gone over the prenuptial agreement that you faxed over, and I must say it is unlike any one I've seen. Did you have a lawyer read this over before you signed it?"

"No, I didn't. I read it but never had anyone look over it until now. At the time, I didn't think I had to." Yara gave a half smile.

"Yes, in my line of work, I see a lot of people make that same mistake. I always tell my clients that if someone sees fit enough to protect themselves via prenup then at the very least, you should protect yourself by having a lawyer read it over and properly explain it to you. In many cases, a prenuptial agreement can be a good thing; however, Mrs. Washington, in your case, it is not."

"There is a part in there about if someone cheats. Can you explain that part to me please?" Yara knew there was a cheating clause; however she was not a lawyer. So, she needed the words on the paper explained to her in layman's terms.

"Yes, you are correct. However, nothing in this prenuptial agreement favors you. It simply states if you divorce Mr. Washington for cheating, you get nothing. If Mr. Washington divorces you for cheating, you get nothing. Mrs. Washington, no matter what happens, this paper says if the two of you divorce for any reason, you are to leave with only what you came into the marriage with."

Yara saw Nathan's mouth moving but heard no words after he said she would get nothing. *How could this mutha-fucka do this to me? As much as I do for him. I run half of the damn laundromats this nigga got, and he wants me to leave with nothing? Oh, fuck him. He ain't 'bout to cheat on me then play me out of what I deserve.*

Without another word, Yara got up from her seat and walked out the office. She was livid and knew she would have to come up with another plan. Tears ran down her face as she made her way to her car. The man she thought she knew, the man she'd married, the man she'd vowed to spend the rest of her life with, was, in fact, someone she didn't know at all. Truce had set things up to where if there was ever a divorce, she would get absolutely nothing. It was narcissism in its finest form, and Yara refused to stand for it.

*Ain't no fuckin' way I'ma let the next bitch get something I helped build. He think he can cheat on me and let another bitch reap the fruits of my labor? He got another fuckin' thing coming,* Yara thought to herself as she made her way out the parking lot. Yara couldn't stop crying. The rage running through her body was unbearable. Before she knew it, she was pulling inside her brother's driveway. She needed to talk to her sister-in-law. Although Fallon was married to her brother, she was Yara's best friend. She called Fallon as soon as she pulled up, letting her know she was outside.

"Hey, girl, what's up?" Fallon asked once Yara walked through the door.

"I need a drink. What you got in here?"

"A drink? Girl, it's eleven thirty in the morning but come on. I got some wine in the kitchen."

"I need something stronger than that, Fallon. Shit fucked up," Yara replied.

Walking into the kitchen, Fallon pulled a bottle of Tito's from the freezer and set it in front of Yara before getting her a glass. Fallon watched as she poured herself a drink, drank it, then poured herself another.

"Girl, what the fuck is going on? Since when do you drink straight and this early?" Fallon asked.

"Truce been cheating on me."

"What? How did you find out?"

"I paid that girl Shelly was talking about. Remember how she was telling us about her paying the girl to get proof of her husband cheating? Well, she gave me her number, and I hired her. But I guess the jokes on me because I just left a lawyer's office, and according to him, if Truce and I get divorced, I don't get anything. No matter what happened to cause the divorce, I can only leave with what I came in with," Yara revealed.

Fallon didn't know what to say. She knew how much work Yara put into each one of Truce's businesses. For her to be left with nothing just didn't seem right. "So, if for any reason the marriage ends, you get nothing?"

"Nothing. He could wake up one day and decide he don't want to be married anymore, and I'ma be ass out. He been cheating on me for I don't know how long, and I gotta just take it?"

"Wait, Yara, I'm confused. You hired someone to basically sleep with your husband, and now you're mad he's sleeping with her? I don't understand."

"Truce has been cheating on me. I know he's been fuckin' other bitches. I just never got any solid proof. That was my whole reason behind hiring her. I thought our prenuptial agreement stated that if he cheated, I could divorce him; however, I was wrong. So, I hired her for nothing."

"What about your online candle store? I know you make good money with that."

"Girl, that shit is pennies compared to the money Truce has. I won't be able to keep up with the lifestyle I'm accustomed to living without his money. Do you know how long it's gonna take me to rebuild? Why the fuck would he play me like this?"

At this point, Fallon needed a drink as well. Hopping up

to grab cranberry juice from the fridge, she poured herself a mixed drink. She took several sips before she spoke again.

"So, what you gon' do, Yara? You just gonna sit around while he sleeps around? Fuck that. You gotta plan your way out now."

"What is there to plan, Fallon? There's no way around it. If I leave, I only get what I came in with, and that's nothing."

"That's why you gotta take it. While y'all are married, you have access to all his accounts, correct?"

"Yes, I do," Yara revealed.

"Good, then start you an account. Start taking money from each account and putting it away for yourself. Do it in small amounts so that he won't notice and let it stack up."

"Yeah, you're right. I could do that as long as he don't catch me. The last thing I want him to think is that I'm stealing from him. That could leave me with nothing as well."

"You just gotta be smart about it. Don't take it out in big amounts, just small amounts every now and then so that he don't notice anything."

"Yeah, you're right. I guess that's the only thing I can do." They sat and spoke for a few moments until Yara's brother, Yaro, came home. Not wanting him to know what was going on, she quickly changed the subject before getting up and leaving altogether. However, she didn't go straight home. She stopped at the liquor store first, needing to have several more drinks in order to deal with the nightmare that was her life.

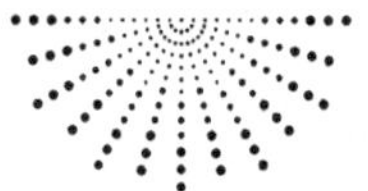

# CHAPTER SIX

Whisper put the finishing touches on her look which was an emerald green, Zara, one piece with her gold Fendi jewelry. She also had a pair of gold Fendi slingbacks and a matching gold bag. Her perfectly painted on red lips looked good with the blonde lace frontal she wore. Her fragrance of choice was YSL Libre which she'd layered with Baccarat Rouge. The smell was intoxicating, and she knew Truce would love it.

Zariah was all ready to go. She was in her car, parked down the street. She would follow them a few places, making sure to take all the pictures Whisper would need. Truce pulled into Whisper's driveway and knocked on the door. When Whisper walked outside, they kissed, and Zariah snapped a picture of it. She followed them to the restaurant and took pictures while they held hands and walked to the door. Zariah followed them the entire night until they made it back to Whisper's house.

"Did you have a good time, baby?" Truce asked once inside Whisper's home.

"I always have a good time anytime I'm with you."

"Good, that's what I like to hear. Why don't we go upstairs, so I can show you something else?"

"How do you know I won't be the one showing you something?" Whisper challenged.

"Shit, show me something then," Truce voiced, walking close to Whisper. Picking her up, he walked her up the stairs and laid her onto her bed. Before he could pull his pants down, Whisper was getting onto her knees. She took him into her mouth and smiled inside when she heard his loud moans.

"Damn, baby, you sucking that dick for Daddy. Get that shit wet."

Whisper kept slurping and sucking like it was a cold popsicle on a hot day. Truce leaned over, unzipping Whisper's one piece, pulling it down and exposing her breasts. He fondled her nipples as she sucked voraciously.

"Damn, baby, this yo dick. Suck that shit like you love it," Truce ordered.

Not wanting to bust before he got to feel the inside of Whisper, Truce pulled himself from her mouth and helped her to her feet. Peeling her clothes off of her body, he tossed them aside before telling Whisper to lay down. She obliged and opened her legs, knowing that Truce's face would be resting there momentarily. Once she felt his tongue, she arched her back and grabbed his head, allowing him to feast on her until he came up. They made love until Truce finally told her he had to go. She knew in the back of her mind that he wouldn't be able to spend the night. However, she wished he could. She wasn't ready to let him go yet. The fact that she knew he was going home to another woman made her sad.

"Why do you have to leave?" Whisper asked.

"I gotta get up early tomorrow morning, babe. But I promise I'll spend the night soon."

Whisper nodded her head, and Truce saw the sadness in her eyes. He didn't want to leave her; however, he knew Yara wouldn't stand for him staying out all night again. He would have to come up with a lie to tell Yara. His main goal was keeping both of his women happy, and that was exactly what he was going to do. Kissing Whisper on the forehead, Truce let himself out.

It was Saturday afternoon, and Yara sat in her living room, watching TV. It was extremely hot outside, with the high being in the low nineties. So, Yara decided to stay in the house in the cool air conditioning. Truce had gotten up early that morning and left the house, telling Yara he was going to check on the laundromats. Her phone rang, and she noticed it was her brother. Swiping the talk button, she answered her phone.

"What up doe?"

"Sis, open the door. I'm outside," Yaro informed.

Getting up from the couch, Yara opened her front door, allowing her brother inside.

"Hey, what's up?" she asked.

"Fallon told me what that nigga, Truce, was on. I knew it was somethin' up with that muthafucka from day one. I mean, he cool, but I know a grimy ass nigga when I see one."

Yara couldn't do anything but shake her head. She loved Fallon, but she didn't understand why her mouth was so big. If Yara wanted her brother to know what was going on, she would have told him herself. Yara sat on her couch while she listened to her brother speak.

"The fact you wouldn't get anything if y'all got divorced is fuckin' crazy. You deserve at least half. I wish you would have gotta lawyer to look over them damn papers before you signed them."

"Yeah, me too. I just didn't think I needed to. I thought Truce would look out for me, but I guess not. What if he leaves me for one of the bitches he fucks, then what? I'ma be ass out with nothing."

"What if I told you I knew a way for you to get everything, and Truce wouldn't be able to stop you? Would you be down for it?"

"What you thinking? Because if it's a way I can do that, then I'm down. I need to be a step ahead. I refuse to have nothing leaving a marriage where I helped build everything." Tears began to form in Yara's eyes as she really thought about the way her husband had played her. He was supposed to be her protector. Instead, he felt more like the enemy to her.

"We can take that nigga out. If he dead, everything goes to you. And I'm sure that nigga got a fat ass insurance policy too. You would get all that if he died," Yaro suggested.

Yara looked up at her brother like he was crazy. She couldn't believe the plan he'd suggested. She wanted to continue the comfortable lifestyle she was used to from being Mrs. Truce Washington. However, killing him to ensure she kept it was a level of crazy Yara wasn't on.

"Boy, you crazy. I'm not trying to go to prison. I only want my just do. And nigga, if I'm in jail, I can't spend the money anyway."

"Yara, you wouldn't go to jail. Our plan would be so airtight that none of us would get caught. Look, just think about it. You don't have to make a decision today. If and when you ready to move forward, come by my house so we can talk. This is something we can never talk about over the phone."

Yara nodded her head before walking Yaro to the door. She didn't give his suggestion another thought. There was no way she was killing her husband. *Imagine me being on a Fatal Attraction episode. That nigga crazy as hell if he think money will turn me into a murderer. I'm way too fine to be in anybody's prison.* Yara sat back down on her couch and continued watching movies for the rest of the afternoon.

· · ·

MONDAY MORNING CAME QUICKLY, AND WHISPER WAS NOT ready for the week. She wanted to take the day off and just relax, but the money she was set to make that day was calling her name. It was going to be a short week for her because Truce had planned them a weekend getaway to Vegas that she was very excited about. So getting up on this Monday morning wouldn't be too bad.

Whisper made her way to the office, walking in and greeting Ari. She'd not been at her desk for five minutes when Ari called her, informing Whisper that she had a client. Whisper wasn't surprised at all when Yara walked through her door.

"Good morning. I was actually going to reach out to you today. I have the pictures that you asked for. Really good ones too in my opinion." Whisper reached into her briefcase and pulled out a manila folder before handing it to Yara. She opened it and began looking through the pictures, her heart breaking with each photo.

"Now, I'm not sure what you would like to do with those photos, but that is indeed the evidence you wanted," Whisper voiced.

"Actually, I was coming here to let you know that these pictures no longer..." Before Yara could finish her sentence, she was interrupted by a knock at the door.

"I'm so sorry, Yara. Give me one moment." Whisper excused herself, walking over to the door and answering it. Ari stood on the other side, speaking quietly so Yara couldn't hear what she was saying.

"Mrs. Washington, just give me a few moments, and I'll be right back." Whisper closed her door, leaving Yara inside her office alone.

Whisper's cell phone rang, and to Yara's surprise, it was Truce. When the ringing stopped, a chime followed shortly after, letting Yara know that he'd texted her. Picking up the phone, Yara opened the text.

**Just wanted to say I love you, and I can't wait for Thursday. We 'bout to fuck Vegas up. Hit me when you not busy, baby.**

Yara's heart sank when she read her husband telling another woman that he loved her. Scrolling through their text thread, she read a few before placing the phone back on the desk. A few moments later, Whisper was walking back into her office.

"I apologize about that. Now, where were we?"

"I was just about to tell you that these pictures didn't matter anyway. After going over our prenuptial agreement, I realized that it was a waste of time hiring you. Thank you but your services are no longer needed. From this point on, stay away from my husband. I will handle this in a different way." Yara walked out of Whisper's office and headed to her car. She was happy that her tears waited until she got inside the car to fall.

*How can he tell her he loves her? He takin' that bitch on trips and everything? How the fuck can he do this to me?* Tears fell from Yara's eyes as she drove home. Her entire spirit had been broken, all from a few words, and she no longer knew what to do. Marrying Truce was supposed to be the best thing that ever happened to her. However, it was starting to look like the worst. Going to her kitchen, Yara grabbed a bottle of Tito's before heading upstairs to her room. She pulled off her clothes before pouring herself a drink and climbing into her bed. The pain she was feeling was unbearable, and she didn't know what she was going to do.

"What the fuck did I do to deserve this shit?" Yara asked aloud. She cried loudly as she felt her heart breaking into a million pieces.

WHISPER AND TRUCE SAT ON HER COUCH, CUDDLED UP, watching the second season of *Your Honor*. Whisper had stopped and picked up some sushi on her way home for them, and they were enjoying their dinner date. Whisper was happy that her dealings with Yara were finally over. Whatever Yara did next was on her. Whisper was just glad she wouldn't have anything to do with it. She could enjoy her man in peace and not have to worry about him finding out she was hired to meet him. Whisper was in love, and she could now enjoy that love without any secrets on her end.

"You got everything you need for Vegas?" Truce asked, wanting to make sure Whisper was ready.

"Yep, I'm all set. I have an appointment to get my hair braided on Wednesday. I know it's gon' be hot as hell in Vegas in the middle of July."

"We 'bout to start traveling a lot more. I'm trying to see

the world with you, baby." Truce smiled, kissing Whisper softly.

"I can't wait," Whisper replied.

"I'm spending the night tonight. I want to be with you tonight," Truce informed.

"I want to be with you every night," Whisper replied.

Yara woke up the next morning and realized Truce had stayed out all night. She knew exactly where he was, and it broke her heart even more. She felt betrayal from them both. She'd paid Whisper to do her job, and instead, she'd fallen in love with Yara's husband.

Getting up from the bed, Yara went to take a shower. She scrubbed herself, trying to wash off all her sorrows. Once out of the shower, she realized she had a missed call from Truce. Calling him, he told her that he'd gotten called on a business trip and wouldn't be back until Monday. The lie rolled off his tongue so easily that it surprised Yara. Yara, not wanting Truce to suspect she knew anything, just saying okay before ending the call. Yara had spent her last night crying over Truce, and as she got inside of her car, she knew exactly what she had to do. Pulling out of her driveway, Yara headed to her brother's house.

"What up doe, sis? What brings you by?" Yaro asked once Yara walked inside.

"Are you here by yourself?"

"Yeah, Fallon went to get her hair done."

"Cool, I wanna talk about that plan you might put together for me. You know what I'm talking about?" Yara asked. She was still trying to talk in code words even though they were face-to-face.

"Hell yeah, I remember. You trying to say you down for that?"

"If I am down for it, what would be the plan? I don't ever want this to come back on me at all. I don't even want to look like a suspect." Yara couldn't believe things had come to this, but hurt people hurt people.

"I got you, sis. Me and my people gon' handle this. They won't ever even know you had something to do with it. The only person that's gon' ever talk to you is me, and you know I ain't gon' say shit."

"He say he got called on a business trip, but I know that's a lie. I think he's at his side piece house," Yara revealed.

"You got the address?"

Yara wrote Whisper's address down on a piece of paper and handed it to Yaro. He told her they would ride out tonight, and he would be by to see her in the morning. Yara agreed before walking out the door and heading back to her house.

"Damn, baby, I get you twice in a row this week?" Whisper joked, coming home from work to see Truce still at her home. He was in the kitchen, seasoning a couple of steaks. Walking up to him, she kissed him softly on the lips.

"Yeah, I just figured I might stay here until we go to Vegas. I like spending time with you and wasn't ready to go home yet."

"That's fine with me. I hate it when you leave anyway. Being around you just makes me feel better."

"Why don't you go upstairs and take your bubble bath? I already ran it for you, and it's nice and hot. Once you get done, dinner will be ready," Truce suggested.

Whisper smiled before heading up to her bathroom. Truce had not only ran her a bubble bath, but he also lit candles all around the bathroom and had soft music playing. He'd set up a relaxing vibe for Whisper, and she loved it. She took her clothes off and eased into the warm, bubbly water before pouring herself a glass of the wine Truce had put to the side.

Just as promised, dinner was ready when Whisper made it back downstairs. They sat at the candlelit table and enjoyed their steak dinner. When they were done, Truce placed the dishes inside the dishwasher before they both headed upstairs. They cuddled in bed as they watched TV.

"WHISPER, GET UP, BABY," TRUCE SPOKE, SHAKING WHISPER out of a sound sleep.

"What time is it?" Whisper asked, wondering why she was being awakened in the middle of the night.

"I think someone is in the house."

With those words, Whisper jumped up. Her heart

pounded as fear set in. She watched as Truce slid into a pair of sweatpants before walking over to the duffle bag he had in the corner of the room. He pulled a gun out before slowly walking to the door.

"Truce, where are you going? Don't leave me in here," Whisper uttered in a low tone.

"Just stay here while I check it out," Truce suggested.

"Hell no. You got the gun, so I'm going with you."

Truce nodded his head and slowly opened the door. They walked down a few steps with the gun leading the way. They heard a few voices whispering, but neither of them could make out what they were saying.

"What's going on? Who are they?" Whisper asked.

"I think they trying to rob you. I can't tell how many of them it is though. I know it's at least two. Is there another way out we can take?"

"Not from up here. The only exit points are downstairs."

"Where is your phone? We need to call the police," Truce suggested.

They both walked back up the stairs quietly and went back into Whisper's room, closing the door behind them. All she could do was drop her head when she realized she'd left her phone downstairs in the kitchen.

"Where is your phone?" Whisper asked.

"It's in the car. We just gon' have to thug it out," Truce spoke.

"What does that mean?"

"Listen, Whisper, just stay behind me. I know this is scary

for you, but know that I'm not going to let anything happen to you. I love you, and I'm gon' protect you with my life. I promise." With those words, Truce opened the door and walked out the room with Whisper close behind him.

They began walking down the steps slowly with the gun leading the way. They'd just gotten halfway down the stairs when a man dressed in all-black appeared at the bottom of the steps. Without hesitation, Truce put two bullets in the man's head. Whisper screamed out in fear when she heard the shots. However, they both continued down the stairs. Bullets began to fly from the back of the house in their direction. Thinking quickly, Truce pulled Whisper down as he shot back, hitting the man that was shooting at them. Running out the front door, they made it to Truce's car before backing out the driveway. As soon as he placed the car in drive, bullets began raining on them, shattering the back windshield.

"Get down!" Truce screamed as he pulled off down the street. Looking into his rearview mirror, he saw the black SUV that was following them, and Truce knew he needed to lose it.

"What's happening? This doesn't seem like a regular robbery to me," Whisper voiced.

"That's because it's not. Somebody gunning for one of us, and it don't look like they stopping until they get what they want. Somebody following us." Truce pointed out. "We gotta get these niggas off us and get somewhere safe. I need to try to figure out who the fuck these muthafuckas are."

Speeding up, Truce turned several corners in an effort to lose the truck. Getting onto the freeway, Truce hit a hundred as he made his way through traffic. He watched as the car sped up behind them. "Put your seat belt on," Truce ordered as he hit one twenty and then one forty before swerving over and getting off at the Michigan Avenue exit. Watching the car that was following them speed past the exit, they drove for several moments before pulling into a Holiday Inn parking lot. Truce parked in the very back, away from anyone else, before they both walked into the hotel.

Whisper had left everything at home, so she didn't have any money or ID, but thankfully, Truce had his wallet. Once they were safely inside the room, they were both able to think. They needed to put their heads together to figure out what was going on.

"Baby, do you have any enemies? Anyone that would want to hurt you? Those people were trying to kill us, and I need to find out who they were," Truce asked.

"No, I don't, but you do."

"What does that mean?" Truce was clearly perplexed and not understanding what Whisper was saying.

"I have to tell you something, but before I do, just know that none of this was fake. I truly do love you, and I could spend the rest of my life showing you that."

"What does that have to do with someone trying to kill us?"

"Your wife hired me to catch you cheating on her. She wanted me to take pictures of us together, so she can have proof you were cheating. She wanted proof so that she could take you to court. I can't lie. I was down with it until I started having feelings for you. Yesterday, she came into my office and said the pictures would no longer work because of the prenup she signed and that she would handle this another way. I had no clue she meant murder," Whisper revealed, silently praying that Truce would still love her after hearing the truth.

For several moments, he didn't say a word. He ran his hands over his head, and Whisper became nervous. She loved Truce and didn't want to lose him. She just wished she'd told him the truth sooner.

"Do you have anything to do with those people shooting at us? Did you know they were coming for me?" Truce stood to his feet, grabbing Whisper with both hands.

"Hell no. I was only supposed to be taking pictures. I'm sorry I didn't tell you sooner, but I had no idea all this shit would happen. Baby, please. You have to believe me. I would never want you to get physically hurt."

Truce looked into Whisper's eyes and knew she was telling the truth. Releasing his grip, he pulled her into his embrace.

"I would never hurt you, baby. I love you," Whisper cried.

"I know, baby, and I love you too. When did Yara hire you?"

"The same day I showed you your house. She met with me right before at another house I was showing. She even told me that you were coming to see a house. She gave me five thousand dollars, and I took it. I had no clue I was going to fall in love with you, and if I did, I never would have done this shit. I'm so sorry, baby."

"It's okay, baby. You telling me now is all I need. But if my wife is in on this, then that means we need to get out this hotel room right now. She's on all my accounts, so I'm sure she knows we were here the moment we checked in."

With those words, Truce grabbed his gun and walked toward the door. Whisper was on his heels as she griped the back of his shirt tightly. Her heart pounded as Truce looked out the peephole before opening the door. Looking down both ends of the hallway, they headed out the room, making their way to the stairs. When they got to the door that led them outside, they paused.

"We gotta be careful going outside. They could already be here. Stay close to me and stay aware of your surroundings," Truce ordered.

Opening the door slowly, they walked outside into the open. It was dark outside, and the cool summer breeze hit their skin, causing goosebumps to form on Whisper's arms. They walked cautiously through the courtyard until they got to the parking lot.

"Truce, it's someone at your car." Whisper noticed before seeing two more men dressed in all-black walking through the parking lot.

They quickly backed up, walking back into the courtyard and back into the hotel. "What the hell are we going to do?" Whisper asked.

"I need to get you somewhere safe, so I can go talk to Yara. This not your drama. I don't want you getting hurt because of me."

"Go see her? Truce, she wants you dead. She got niggas out here gunnin' for you. Why would you go talk to her? She don't want to talk. She wants you dead."

"What you want me to do, keep running? Nah, that's not even my style. I like to handle shit straight up, and I need to handle this shit."

"Why can't you just call her and talk to her? Truce, I don't know what I would do if something happened to you. Baby, please," Whisper pleaded.

Truce saw the worry in her face and knew that it was sincere. He saw that she was scared, and he knew he would need to give her some reassurance.

"Okay, Whisper. I'll call her, but if an over the phone conversation can't handle this, then I'm going to see her. And I still need to get you somewhere safe. I can't handle this shit and worry about your safety at the same time. I don't have no cash, and my credit and debit cards will lead her right to us. I just need a second to think."

As if a lightbulb had gone off in Whisper's head, she remembered the house she showed in Westland. All she needed to do was log into her work email and get the code to the house. She informed Truce about the house, letting him know that would be a safe place to go overnight. There was nobody due at the house until Monday morning, and Whisper knew no one would look for them there.

"Okay, we just gotta get to my car without them seeing us. Let's give it a few minutes and see if they leave the parking lot," Truce suggested.

They stood in the hallway for several minutes before walking back into the courtyard. They swiftly walked through the sidewalk until they made it to the parking lot. Truce looked around cautiously, not seeing anyone in the parking lot.

"They must be in the hotel. Hurry up. Let's get to the car."

Making a run for it, they made it to Truce's car and pulled out of the parking lot before anyone else saw them. Truce was able to breathe a sigh of relief as they made their way down Michigan Avenue. Pulling into the neighborhood, Whisper pointed out the house. Truce pulled into the driveway, and Whisper got out of the car. She put the code into the garage, allowing the door to open. Truce pulled his car into the garage before they both went into the house.

"We should be safe here for the next few nights. This house isn't scheduled to be shown for a few days."

Whisper looked over at the clock and saw it was almost five in the morning. The sun would be coming up soon, and she thought they would be safe in the daylight. *Ain't nobody coming to shoot at us in broad daylight, so we can breathe easy for a little while,* Whisper thought. Thankfully, the house had already been staged for a future viewing, so there was already furniture inside the home.

"When are you going to call Yara?" Whisper questioned as she took a seat on the couch.

"I'll give it a few hours then call her. I'm not too sure if speaking with her over the phone will give me the outcome I want, but I'm willing to try it for you. But, Whisper, if calling her don't stop them from coming after me, I need you to understand that I will show my face. Ain't no bitch in me, so whoever she hired is gon' have to meet me straight up."

Whisper nodded her head. As much as she didn't want Truce to go, she knew there was nothing she could do to stop him. That was his wife that was doing this to him. Whisper wanted to protect her man. She knew she had no claim to him when it came to Yara; however, wife or not, Whisper would kill Yara with her bare hands if she did anything to cause harm to Truce.

A few hours later, Truce decided it was time to call Yara. As mad as he was that she would resort to trying to kill him for his money, he wanted to talk to her and see where her head was at. Maybe if he spoke to her, he could talk her out of this. Letting Whisper know he was about to make the call, he walked into one of the back bedrooms, so he would have some privacy. The phone rang several times before she answered.

"Yara, what you doing? You got niggas shooting at me? I thought you loved me, my baby?"

"Where you at? With that bitch, Whisper, huh? I thought you loved me. Instead, you threw us away for some quick pussy. Then, on top of that, this prenup is bullshit. I helped you with every company you have, and in the prenup, I get nothing? You want me to leave with the same shit I came in with? You wouldn't even be able to run them fuckin' businesses if it wasn't for me."

"So, my life is just worth money to you? So, you gon' what? Kill me and live happily ever after with my money? Do you really think any money is going to come to you if you kill me? How did we get here, Yara? We took vows, baby. I didn't think we would ever be apart, so I didn't give a fuck about the prenup. Me asking you to sign it was a test, a test that I thought you passed until now."

"Did you give a fuck about our vows when you were out fuckin' yo side bitches? Or do our vows only apply to me?" Yara was in rare form, and Truce didn't know how to take it. He couldn't believe his once loving wife was acting so cold to him.

"I don't have a side bitch, Yara."

"Really? So, you're not with Whisper right now? That's whose house you were at when my people came for you. And I know you left together, so where is she? See, I think you trying to play me for a fool. I know you with her, so you better enjoy that shit. My people on their way right now. Or did you forget that I have your location?"

As soon as Yara said those words, Truce ran into the living room where Whisper was. He opened his mouth to speak, but before he could, a brick was thrown into the window. It was followed by a Malakoff cocktail, which set the curtains on fire immediately. Whisper looked over in shock as the flames grew.

"Whisper, come on. We gotta go!" Truce yelled.

Whisper screamed out in fear, jumping up from the couch and running toward Truce. They'd just made it to the kitchen when they heard gunshots. Whisper screamed out in fear, knowing they'd been found. Running into the garage, Whisper got into the car and started it while Truce opened the door. As quickly as he could, Truce peeled out of the driveway, speeding down the street. Bullets followed them, hitting the car as they drove off. There was so much damage to the car that Truce knew they couldn't continue to drive it. The car was starting to run hot, and Truce knew he would have to pull over.

"What you doing?" Whisper asked as Truce pulled the car over. Once she noticed the smoke coming from the hood, she knew exactly what was wrong.

"We gotta find another car." Truce looked around, hoping he'd lost any tails they might have had. When he didn't see anyone, he got out the car, motioning for Whisper to follow him. Leaving his phone inside the car, he grabbed a small black bag out of the trunk before they began walking down the street.

"Baby, what are we going to do? We can't be out here in the open like this." Whisper was nervous as she continuously looked over her shoulder.

"I know, baby. We gotta find a car," Truce informed.

Walking over to an older model black Jeep, Truce looked around before pulling a screwdriver from the small bag and popping the lock. Once the door was open, he got in before unlocking the passenger door for Whisper. It only took

Truce a few minutes to fiddle with the wires before the car started. Truce pulled off before the owners knew the car had even been stolen. They rode in silence for several moments before Truce began speaking.

"I'm going to speak to Yara face-to-face. I'm not 'bout to run from her or any nigga she got gunnin' for me. If she wanna take me out, she gon' have to do it straight up."

"Truce, why can't we just call the police and let them handle it? You see Yara ain't lettin' up, so what do you think she gon' do to you when you show your face?"

"I'm not calling no damn police. Fuck I look like? I'm 'bout to go talk to this bitch straight up. But before I do, I gotta take you somewhere safe. Do you have anywhere you can go?"

Whisper didn't want Truce to go, but she knew there was nothing she could do to stop him. So, with nothing else to say, Whisper directed Truce to Zariah's house. They arrived at Zariah's house about fifteen minutes later.

"Please be careful, Truce. How am I going to know that you're alright?"

"I'm gonna call you after I talk to her. I'ma be good, baby. Don't worry about me," Truce replied.

Whisper nodded her head before leaning over and kissing Truce. Getting out of the car, she walked up to Zariah's door before knocking. Truce waited for Whisper to walk inside before he pulled off.

"Hey, girl, what's up with you? You didn't work today?" Zariah asked once Whisper was inside.

"Z, I need your gun and your car," Whisper stated.

"My gun? Bitch, what the fuck are you talking about?" Zariah was confused by her friend's request and wanted to ensure that she heard her correctly.

"Please, Z, I don't have time to explain myself. And the less you know, the better. I wouldn't ask you if it wasn't an emergency."

Zariah looked at Whisper and saw the desperation in her eyes. Zariah didn't speak, just nodded her head before walking upstairs to retrieve her gun. When she came back, she handed both the gun and her key fob to Whisper.

"Thank you, bestie. I'll be back as soon as I can."

With those words, Whisper ran out the door. She knew Truce was going to meet Yara at their house, and since she'd sold it to them, Whisper knew exactly where it was. She did a hundred down 94, trying to get there at the same time that Truce did. Whisper didn't have a plan, but she knew she would do anything to ensure Truce came out of this alive. She was taking a huge risk going up against his wife, but Whisper didn't care. She loved Truce and wouldn't be able to live with herself if anything were to happen to him.

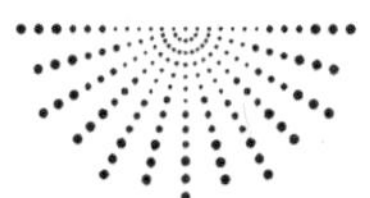

# CHAPTER SEVEN

When Whisper pulled up to the house, she saw that the car Truce had been driving was already parked outside, but he wasn't in it. Getting out the car, gun in hand, she made her way to the door. She turned the knob and like she knew it would be, the door was locked. She wanted to try the code but knew that it had been changed. She also knew that if she put the wrong code in, the alarm would sound and bring unwanted attention to her presence.

Making her way around the back of the house, she realized the garage door was slightly open. Running over, she attempted to push the garage door up, but it would go any farther. Knowing she had no other way inside, Whisper put her gun in her waistline before crawling under the door. As soon as she walked into the door that led in the house, she heard Yara and Truce arguing. Making her way through the house, she followed their voices until she got upstairs to the master bedroom. She stood at the door, listening to their words.

"This is all about money. You ain't never gave a fuck about me. You gon' kill me over some money that I made. How the fuck does that work? You really had niggas on my head, and you supposed to be my wife," Truce yelled.

"You been cheating on me for as long as we been married. But I guess you thought I didn't know. Then you had the nerve to really be spending time with that bitch. You took that hoe on trips and spent the night with her. And I was just supposed to sit back and take it? I'm not a fuckin' robot, Truce. I have feelings!"

Whisper could hear the pain in her voice, and she sympathized with her. She knew the pain of being hurt by a man and the outlandish things a woman could do afterwards. However, Truce was off limits, and Whisper refused to allow Yara to turn him into the next *Fatal Attraction* episode. She held her gun at her side as she continued to listen to their conversation.

"You hired her! You paid her to fuck with me. Now you mad that I fell in love with her? This was your doing. It wouldn't even be a her if it wasn't for you. I don't understand you at all, and I really think you should go seek mental help."

"Oh, so you love her?" Yara asked, fighting back tears. She bit her bottom lip as her chest fell in defeat.

"Yes, I do. I didn't mean for this to happen, but it did.

Even if I didn't love her, I still wouldn't be with you after this. You put a price on my head, Yara. It's no coming back from this. We over."

Truce was out done. Although he was angry, he was more hurt than anything. No matter what else he did, he always loved Yara and would have protected her with his life. Yet she was willing to take his just for a payday. He'd taken vows to love and protect Yara, while she'd gone against those very vows and tried to put a bullet in him.

"You think I put in all this work to let you just walk away? You fuckin' crazy if you think that. The only place you will be going is to hell if you leave me now." Yara grabbed her gun before aiming it at Truce. Tears ran down her face as she shook in anger. She couldn't believe her husband was standing in front of her, telling her he was in love with another woman and leaving her. Yara's entire plan had back-fired, and she felt stupid for even letting that happen. Knowing it was no turning back, Yara continued to aim the gun at him.

"I can't let you do that, Truce. If you leave here today, it won't be with another bitch. You leave here, it's gon' be in a fuckin' body bag."

"So, you gone kill me right here? Man, Yara, put that fuckin' gun down." Truce chuckled, calling Yara's bluff. "If you could pull that trigger yourself, you would have done it already. But you didn't. You had to hire other people to kill me because you knew you wouldn't be able to do that shit yourself. Put the fucking gun down, Yara! You shoot me right here and you know them nosy ass neighbors gon' call the police," Truce yelled.

Whisper heard Truce's words and immediately wanted to run into the room. However, she knew they didn't know she was even in the house. She feared that if she ran inside the room and startled Yara, she would shoot Truce out of fear. Her heart pounded as her palms began to sweat. She wanted to run inside the room blasting, letting Yara know she didn't play about Truce. She wanted to let Yara know that Truce was her man, and she would do anything to protect him. Instead, she stood at the door and continued to listen in.

"Oh, you think I won't do that jail time, nigga? You played me the entire time when you could have left me alone. You wanted me, remember? You did this shit, nigga, and now you have to suffer the consequences. You gon' learn not to fuck with people's feelings."

"You can't be fuckin' serious. I'm…"

Before Truce could finish his sentence, Yara pulled the trigger, allowing the gun to go off. As soon as Whisper heard the shot, she ran through the door with her gun aimed and ready to shoot. She saw Yara standing there with the gun still smoking. Without any words, Whisper shot twice with one of the bullets hitting Yara in the chest.

"Noooo!" Truce yelled, catching Yara before she hit the floor.

Whisper stood there with her mouth open as she looked over at Truce. Besides being shot in the arm, he was fine. When Whisper heard the gunshot, she'd though Truce was dead, so she came in on instinct. If she would have just waited a few more seconds, she would have realized that Truce was indeed still alive.

"I thought she killed you! I heard the shot. I didn't know. Oh, my God, is she okay?" Whisper was stumbling over her words as she spoke. Tears fell from her face as she looked down at Truce cradling Yara. Even after she'd tried to kill him, he was still crying for her. Blood formed a stain onto Yara's light blue shirt, and Truce knew it was bad.

"Give me the gun and get outta here," Truce said in a low tone.

"What do you mean?" Whisper asked, confused.

"Give me the fuckin' gun and get the hell outta here," Truce reiterated. He wanted Whisper to leave the house before the police came. He'd dropped her off at her friend's house, not knowing she would follow him. His heart raced as he tried to put together a story. Grabbing Yara's phone, he called the police, trying to get her help. Even after Yara tried to kill him, he didn't want her to die. He said a silent prayer to God, hoping she would be okay.

Whisper handed Truce her gun before running out of the house. Truce held Yara in his arms as he tried to speak life into her. Her blood was seeping through his fingers as he tried to apply pressure to her wound. "Please, Yara, don't die. I can't let this shit end like this. Just hold on, baby. They almost here."

"I don't wanna die, Truce. Please help me," Yara cried.

"Help is on the way, baby. Just please hold on."

Truce looked down at Yara, who was now in and out of consciousness, and he continued to coach her to stay awake. A few moments later, Truce heard a hard knock at the door and knew it was the police. Lying Yara flat on the floor, he ran downstairs to let them inside. He led the paramedics up to their room where Yara was still on the floor. An officer walked in after them, pulling Truce to the side for questioning.

"Mister?"

"Washington," Truce replied.

"Mr. Washington, I'm Officer Schmitt. Can you tell me what happened here today?" the officer asked.

"My wife has been shot. I just want them to help her. I need to make sure she's okay. Please help her. She can't die."

"I can assure you the paramedics are doing everything they can, and she will be transported to the hospital. But I need you to work with me. I know this might be hard, but if we are going to get the person that shot your wife, you're going to have to answer some questions," Officer Schmitt confirmed.

"I shot my wife," Truce revealed as he held his head low. The words didn't even sound believable coming from his mouth, but there was no way he was going to give up Whisper. As crazy as the situation was, and as much as he prayed Yara pulled through, he didn't blame Whisper. He knew she was only trying to help, and her love for him made her want to protect him. Truce just wished it would have happened differently.

"Did you say you shot your wife?" the officer asked, making sure he'd heard Truce correctly.

"Yes, but in self-defense. She has been trying to kill me, which I have proof of. I came home to try to talk to her, thinking that if I could just speak with her face-to-face, it would calm everything down. But I was clearly wrong about that. In the middle of us talking, she ended up pulling a gun on me. She shot twice, and I reacted off instinct and shot as well."

The officer looked at Truce, stunned at how easy he'd just made his job. While the paramedics were wheeling Yara out into the ambulance, Officer Schmitt was putting handcuffs on Truce.

"I've been shot, and I need medical attention," Truce informed.

"We will get you that, but these handcuffs are protocol."

Whisper watched on in tears, not knowing what to do as the paramedics wheeled Yara out to the ambulance. Although Truce had told her to leave, she couldn't. There was no way Whisper could just leave him without knowing what was going to happen next. A few moments later, she saw Truce being escorted to a police car in handcuffs. Her heart sank, knowing Truce was about to go to jail. She wanted to jump out the car and run to him, but she knew she couldn't. Right before they placed him inside the police car, their eyes locked. Truce mouthed the words, "I love you. Drive away."

Whisper, tears streaming down her faced, mouthed, "I

love you too." She then placed the car in drive and pulled off. She prayed that Truce would call her and tell her what to do. She wanted to be there for him because she knew it was her fault this was happening in the first place. Her tears began to flow rapidly, and the bright morning sun hit her eyes. Pulling over, Whisper broke down. The love that she'd waited to receive was about to be ripped away from her. She wept loudly, hitting the steering wheel in frustration.

"Fuck!" she yelled out loud. "Get yourself together."

With that, Whisper wiped her tears and drove back to Zariah's house. She got out the car, walled into the unlocked house, and fell into her best friend's arms.

"What's wrong?" Zariah asked, hugging Whisper tightly.

Whisper sat down on the couch with Zariah following behind her. She exposed her entire self to her best friend in one sitting, and Zariah was shocked to say the least. Zariah sat there, trying to process everything Whisper was telling her. She had no idea about the side hustle Whisper had, not to mention the fact that Truce had been married the entire time and Whisper knew.

"What are you going to do?" Zariah asked.

"Right now, I just have to wait for Truce. There's no way I can leave him in jail for something I did. I have to find him a lawyer and be by his side at every trial. I just pray Yara doesn't die."

"I just don't know what to say, Whisper. I know you got to be scared as hell. But I can help you find him a lawyer.

There's quite a few big names that come through my restaurant, and I know a couple of them personally."

"Thank you so much, Zariah. I really appreciate that. Can I use your bathroom? I need a hot shower and a change of clothes," Whisper asked, looking down at the small shorts and white tank top she had on.

"Of course. You go ahead and take a shower and help yourself to anything inside my closet. It's also brand new underwear inside a bag in my bottom drawer. I'll call around to a few lawyers and see who can take his case."

Whisper thanked Zariah again before making her way to the bathroom. She wished she had a time machine so that she could go back and do things differently. She would have met Truce in a different way and never taken the offer from his wife. She prayed that this would all work out for the good as she let the water run down her body. Thoughts of Truce ran through her mind, and she hoped the lawyer would be able to get him off.

# CHAPTER EIGHT

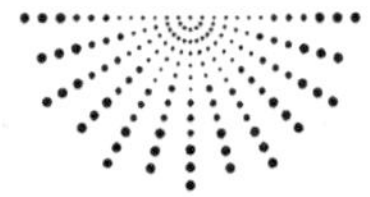



Whisper placed lotion all over her body before stepping into a white dress she'd picked up from Zara. It was a short, spaghetti strapped dress that stopped a few inches above Whisper's knees. The dress was fitted at the top, cinched at her waist, and flared out at the bottom. Whisper kept on her same signature jewelry, only this time, she tied a navy-blue and white Versace scarf around her neck. It was late July, and the news reported a high of ninety degrees. Knowing that it would be extremely hot, Whisper wanted to go with a fresh scent when choosing her fragrance of the day. So, she went with Delina Exclusif.

Whisper slid into her navy-blue Christian Louboutins and grabbed her purse before heading out the door.

Truce's verdict was being read, and she wanted to be one of the first people inside the courtroom. The trail had been going on for an entire year, and Truce had been denied bail. Zariah had put Whisper in contact with a great lawyer, and she just prayed that all his arguments and the evidence presented would be enough for a not guilty verdict. Yara had indeed lived, making Truce's charges attempted murder and assault with a deadly weapon. However, his lawyer was adamant that they would win the case. Whisper walked into the courtroom and took a seat in the front. She wanted Truce to see her face the moment he walked inside.

Truce smiled at Whisper, mouthing the words, "I love you," before sitting down. Truce was nervous, and although the courtroom was air conditioned, he was sweating. They all stood to their feet as the judge walked in. Everyone in the courtroom took their seats once the judge was finally seated. Both the defense and the prosecution gave their final statements before the jurors went in for deliberation. The court was in recess, and Whisper walked into the bathroom. Walking out of the stall, she headed to the sink to wash her hands. As she looked into the mirror, she saw Yara walking out of one of the stalls behind her. Whisper's eyes widened as they locked with Yara. She was shocked to see her, not thinking she would be anywhere near Truce's trial.

"I see you still running behind my husband. You ain't

learned yo lesson yet, huh?" Yara asked, walking up to Whisper.

"He's only still your husband because he's in jail. As soon as he gets out of here, he gon' be giving yo ass divorce papers. Truce is my man, and we both know it. You see what happened the last time you came for him, so you might want to slow down. Looks to me that you the one that hasn't learned their lesson."

Whisper wasn't going to back down. She wanted Yara to know she was still standing on business when it came to Truce, and she always would. Yara put no fear in Whisper's heart, and she wanted her to know that.

"Yeah, we gon' see, bitch," Yara threatened.

Yara washed her hands before walking out of the bathroom, leaving Whisper standing there. Whisper was dumbfounded at the nerve of her. She didn't even love Truce. It had been Yara that tried to kill him in the first place. Because of Yara, Truce was fighting for his freedom right now.

Walking out of the courthouse, Whisper decided to walk down to the sandwich shop that was on the corner. It was almost one in the afternoon, and she hadn't eaten anything. She had over an hour to kill with court not due to resume until two. Sitting down at the table, she looked over the menu. She'd just placed her order when Yara walked into the front door. *Man, what the fuck? I just can't get away from this bitch,* Whisper thought to herself as she rolled her eyes. Yara, seeing Whisper sitting at a table alone, walked over to her and took a seat.

"What do you want now, Yara?"

"Relax, I come in peace. I didn't want to wait the fifteen minutes for a table, so I told them I was with you. We don't even have to speak. We can just eat in silence."

Whisper nodded her head. At the very least, Whisper could allow her to sit and eat. She was the one who shot the woman in her chest. Although Whisper didn't care for Yara at all, she'd also introduced her to the love of her life. So, with that, they sat down and ate lunch together without saying a word.

Walking back into the courtroom, Whisper took her seat in the front row as everyone else reentered the courtroom. The verdict was in, and the foreman stood to deliver it. When he said they'd found Truce not guilty on all counts, tears of joy ran down Whisper's face. Her man was coming home, and she couldn't have been happier about it.

It took them a few hours to process Truce out of the system, but when they did, Whisper was right there waiting. She ran to him, and he wrapped his strong arms around her. It had been a year since he'd held her in his arms, and it felt good to Truce. Whisper had held him down for the entire year he'd been locked up, and that was a type of loyalty Truce couldn't help but respect. He knew her love for him was strong, and that made his love for her even stronger.

"Let's go home, baby," Truce suggested.

Nodding her head, they got into Whisper's car, and she pulled off. When they made it to Whisper's brand-new, four-bedroom home, it was forty-five minutes later. She pulled into her garage, and they both walked inside the house.

"What you want to do for the rest of the night?" Whisper asked.

Truce walked over to Whisper, wrapping his arms around her waist and pulling her closer. "You. I want to do you for the rest of the night. I've missed you more than you could ever know, and I need to feel you right now."

Truce kissed Whisper's lips softly, and her entire body melted. She'd missed Truce too and wanted nothing more than to feel his body on hers. Grabbing Truce's hand, she led him up to the master bedroom. Walking into the en-suite bathroom, she turned on the shower before they both undressed. Stepping into the shower, they washed each other while engaging in sweet kisses.

Once out of the shower, they made their way to the bedroom, making love over and over until they were both spent. At the end of their four hour long session, they were both hungry. It was after midnight, and they knew nothing worth eating was open that late. With that, Whisper decided to go into the kitchen and cook, making a quick pasta salad they both enjoyed. They then headed back to the bedroom where they continued to please each other.

That next morning, Truce woke up, deciding he wanted to barbecue by the pool and have some fun in the sun with his lady. It was a Saturday morning, and he'd missed so many of them being locked in a cell for the past year. Getting dressed, Truce made a trip to the grocery store to pick up everything he would need for the dinner he wanted to prepare.

By the time he returned to the house, Whisper was up and dressed for the day. Truce informed her of the plans he'd made for them for the day, and Whisper was more than down for it. She went right into the kitchen and began seasoning the meat Truce would put on the grill. Whisper connected her phone to her Bluetooth speaker and allowed the nineties R&B to blare through the house. Truce had also bought sides for them to prepare. It was a full on summer cookout, even if it was just the two of them.

Once the meat was seasoned, Whisper started on the sides. When she was done, she went upstairs and changed into her swimsuit before joining Truce in the backyard.

"Look at yo sexy ass," Truce complimented, kissing Whisper on the lips when she walked out in her Pucci two-piece.

"Come get in the pool with me while you wait on them ribs to smoke," Whisper suggested.

Truce obliged, easing himself down into the water. Truce was having a wonderful time with the love of his life. The music that was bumping through the speaker was adding a good vibe to the festivities.

"You wanna have a couple drinks? I got everything we need to mix us up anything we want," Truce suggested.

"Hell yeah, it's a party. Let's get that liquor flowing." Whisper laughed.

Getting out of the pool, they wrapped themselves in

towels before heading into the kitchen. Truce grabbed himself a beer and handed Whisper a spiked lemonade, letting her know that he'd also gotten liquor for mixed drinks whenever she was ready for one. They finished cooking before making their plates and taking them out to the back patio table, continuing to enjoy the outdoors. They ate their food and had several more drinks as they enjoyed good music. Even with it just being the two of them, they partied like they were with a crowd full of people and had fun doing so. By the time the sun went down, they were both a bit tipsy.

Making their way back into the house once the mosquitoes began biting too much, they both took a shower before they both grabbed a mixed drink. They made their way to the living room, cups in hand, as they sat on the couch. Whisper turned on Netflix and began scrolling.

"I'm going to file for divorce Monday morning. I already have a lawyer in mind and everything. I'm ready for it to be me and you forever," Truce announced.

Whisper couldn't do anything but smile. Truce was showing her so much love, and she was enjoying every moment of it. They had just agreed on a movie to watch when someone knocked on the door. "I'll get it," Truce offered, getting up from the couch.

Whisper paused the movie, not wanting Truce to miss the beginning. A few moments later, she heard a gunshot. Jumping up, Whisper ran to the door where she saw Truce lying on the floor with a bullet to his head.

"Truce, please no! Oh, my God! Baby, please don't do this!" she screamed, running over to him. Blood was all over her walls and floor, and the hole in Truce's head let her know he was already dead. Looking out the door, she saw a person in all-black run to a car before pulling off down the street. She rushed to grab her cell phone and called for help, but it was too late. Truce was pronounced dead on arrival.

It had been weeks since Truce's passing, and Whisper had finally gone back to work. Yara had Truce cremated, so there wasn't even a service to celebrate his life. Because he was killed before he could file for divorce, Yara was able to make all plans regarding Truce's services. Whisper sat in her office, thinking about the past year of her life. She'd found a man that had genuinely loved her, and now, he was gone. Truce would have done anything for Whisper, and she knew it. There was no way around it. Whisper was going to truly miss Truce and forever hold on to the memories they shared. Sitting at her desk in deep thought, she was interrupted when Ari informed her that a client was here to see her.

"Let them in," Whisper confirmed.

Ari walked out, leaving the door open with the client walking right in, closing the door behind her. Yara took a seat in one of the chairs at Whisper's desk.

"Hello, Yara, what can I do for you now?" Whisper asked.

"I was just coming to give you your cut, girl. I got the check from the insurance company a few days ago, so I got your money. I want to thank you for everything you did for me because I know I wouldn't have been able to do any of this without you. It was times you had me thinking that you were in love with his ass. Then, when you shot me, you took it to another level. Girl, what if you would have killed me?"

"Yara, as you can see, I'm an excellent shot. I knew exactly what I was doing. I needed to make everything look real. But you, Miss Let Me Set the Damn House on Fire, what the hell was that shit about? I told you it was a house that was on the market. I'm so glad that shit didn't come back on me. I could have lost my job."

"Nah, don't blame me for that. I had no clue Yaro was gonna be setting fire to shit." Yara laughed.

"Girl, that shit almost made me break character and bust our whole shit up. You gotta warn me when he gon' do some crazy shit like that. That was something I wasn't expecting."

Yara nodded her head as she continued to laugh. She'd enjoyed doing business with Whisper and would recommend her services to anyone interested. Because of Whisper, her cheating husband was out of her life, and she was now five million dollars richer. Not to mention, there were the laundromats and parking lot that Yara now owned. Everything that Truce had now belonged to her, and she knew she deserved it. Yara would be set for life, and none of it would have been possible without the help of Whisper. Reaching down to her side, Yara picked the briefcase up and placed it onto Whisper's desk before opening it.

"Five hundred thousand, all cash. Just as we talked about," Yara revealed.

Whisper nodded her head and smiled as she looked down at the bills, rubbing her hands together. Even though it had taken a year of her life, the payout of the job was well worth it. She said her goodbyes to Yara, thanking her for her business, before closing the briefcase and placing it under her desk. She couldn't wait for her next job and hoped it would be an even bigger payout than the last.

The End.

# REVIEW

Did you enjoy the read?
Let us know how much by leaving us a review on Amazon
and Goodreads.

# OTHER BOOKS BY

**<u>URBAN AINT DEAD</u>**

Tales 4rm Da Dale

The Hottest Summer Ever

Hittin' Licks For The Holidays: Atlanta

Wet Dreams On Lockdown: The Nurse

How To Publish A Book From Prison

By **Elijah R. Freeman**

Despite The Odds

By **Juhnell Morgan**

Good Girls Gone Rogue

Good Girls Gone Rouge 2

By **Manny Black**

Hittaz

Hittaz 2

Hittaz 3

Hittaz 4

Coldhearted

By **Lou Garden Price, Sr.**

Charge It To The Game

Charge It To The Game 2

A Summer To Remember With My Hitta

Snatched Up By A Hitta

Santa Sent Me A Real One For Christmas

Wet Dreams on Lockdown: The Unit Manager

Thug Me The Right Way 2

Thug Me The Right Way 3

Seizing A Gangsta's Heart for the Summer

By **Nai**

A Setup For Revenge

Wet Dreams On Lockdown: The Librarian

By **Ashley Williams**

Ridin' For You

Ridin' For You, Too

Trickin' on a Heaux for Christmas: A BBW Love Story

Homie Hoppin' For The Holidays

Wet Dreams on Lockdown: The Female C.O

Letters Of His Love

By **Telia Teanna**

The State's Witness

The State's Witness 2

The State's Witness 3

This Time Won't You Save Me

This Time Won't You Save Me 2

By **Kyiris Ashley**

Stuck In The Trenches

Stuck In The Trenches 2

By **Huff Tha Great**

The Swipe

The Swipe 2

By **Toōla**

Melted the Heart of a Menace

Wet Dreams On Lockdown: Lieutenant Grace

**By P. Wise**

Merry Trapmas: Ice & Frost

By **Mia Sky**

Thug Me The Right Way

By **DiamondATL & Nai**

Atlantastan

By **Chris Green**

IN The Streetz

By **Tron Hill**

Wet Dreams on Lockdown: The Male C.O
By **Tamyra Griffin**

Wet Dreams On Lockdown: The Counselor
By **Paris Iman**

Wet Dreams On Lockdown: The Warden
By **Shawnice**

Wet Dreams On Lockdown: The Captain
By **TN Jones**

BOOKS BY


URBAN AINT DEAD's C.E.O

**<u>Elijah R. Freeman</u>**


Triggadale

Triggadale 2

Triggadale 3


Tales 4rm Da Dale

The Hottest Summer Ever


Murda Was The Case

Murda Was The Case 2

Murda Was The Case 3


Hittin' Licks For The Holidays: Atlanta


Wet Dreams On Lockdown: The Nurse


How To Publish A Book From Prison

# STAY CONNECTED

Follow
**Elijah R. Freeman**
On Social Media
FB: Elijah R. Freeman
IG: @the_future_of_urban_fiction